Wayward Soul

By L.D. Greenwood

Wayward Soul, Book One of the Wayward Gods Trilogy

By L.D. Greenwood

I greatly appreciate you taking the time to read my work. Please consider leaving a review wherever you bought the book, or telling your friends about it, to help spread the word.
Thank you for supporting me.

To my mother, the real Ellie. Thank you for always believing in me.

CHAPTER ONE

It was cold in the house and I frowned in confusion. I paused in the doorway, remembering Jana's blue car in the driveway. My little sister was a bit of a baby when it came to the temperature. She liked the fire roaring and the heater turned up full blast, even though she was the one paying the electric bill because of it.

I dropped my keys into the wooden bowl on the bookshelf by the door and removed my red scarf and white knit hat. I took off my snow-covered boots and left them on the super-absorbent mat by the door, before padding forward in socked feet.

"Jana!" I called out, wondering where she was. "I'm home."

The little, two-story structure was cozy, built in the late 1990's in an area that was trying to look Victorian. The living room had high ceilings, and the large French doors that led to the back porch let in faint light from the street.

I reached for the light-switch, but the faintest whiff of an unfamiliar scent made me hesitate. Jana didn't need me to protect her, but the scent coming to me from the dark living room was metallic; it reminded

3

me of blood.

My heart started beating faster, and I resisted the urge to call out. Jana was fine. She had to be fine. She was a witch, and as such, she could protect herself. Besides, I was a witch too, and I wouldn't be afraid in my own home.

Holding fast to that confidence, I reached out and flicked the switch.

The beige carpet was red, drenched with blood, and so was my sister.

She was strewn across the floor, her limbs all akimbo. Her blonde hair was spread out in a perfect half-moon, around her face. It was draped over her outstretched arm, but it couldn't hide the deep cuts on her forearm, running from her elbow to her wrist. The cuts were so deep that I could see hints of white bone.

From where I stood at the threshold, the girl's face was hidden from me, but I'd recognize Jana's lithe form anywhere. I took a step forward involuntarily, my heart aching with a pain that I hadn't yet acknowledged.

I don't know how long I stood there with my heart beating loudly in my ears and the edges of my vision going black, but eventually I realized I wasn't alone with Jana's body. There was a presence in the back corner, hugging the shadows and trying to stay unobtrusive, as it put something in a bottle.

I looked up, and found myself staring into the eyes of a man. No, it wasn't a man. It was a siekewa, a soul dealer. He was carefully dropping a silvery substance into a dark vial. Each movement was practiced, and even though I'd never seen a soul's energy without a body before, I knew it exactly for what it was.

Immediately I reached for the magic stored in the sapphire ring on my right hand. The power burned through me, strengthened by my fear.

"Let go of my sister's soul, you monster!" I shouted, moving forward and holding my now-glowing hands in front of me.

It looked at me in surprise. Its blue eyes were icy, and the color seemed to spread the chill into my bones. I pulled more power out of my ring, burning the death from his gaze out of my lungs.

It looked like a man, but I tried not to think of him as one. He was beautiful in his surprise, his sculpted face almost seeming a mask. His mouth was a perfect "O" and his long lashes were dark against his alabaster skin.

"You can see me," he mused, his hands curling around the black bottle that was glowing faintly. His voice was beautiful, but it made my skin crawl to hear something so evil speaking to me.

"Monster," I hissed, feeling my long auburn hair start to float in the aura my magic created. "Let my sister's soul go. It doesn't belong to you."

"Actually," he said, his baritone voice smug, "it does. Jana and I have a pre-existing arrangement. She didn't deliver on her end of the bargain, so her life and her soul are forfeit."

"Liar! Jana would never work with a siekewa." I took a confident step forward, my skin glowing with power. He would give back Jana's soul or I would break his human form and take it from him.

"She wanted to be stronger," he said, waving his hand to make a long scroll appear in front of him. With a flick of his wrist, it unfurled and floated towards me. It was a contract.

"She was tired of living in your shadow. I can see why. You are... quite a specimen."

His compliment made me sick, but the heavy

words at the end of the scroll made me sicker.

If I cannot complete the task outlined above, I forfeit my soul.

And there, in painfully familiar handwriting, was Jana's name, written in blood.

My confidence faltered, and the extra power flowed seamlessly back into my ring. My hair fell back around my shoulders, frizzy from the magic's charge.

"I asked her for a simple thing too, but she decided she didn't want to do it anymore. She asked for me to take back the power I gave her, but the contract is quite clear," he said, snapping his fingers.

The scroll rolled back up and vanished with a small pop. I didn't even flinch. I stared at Jana's body, my hands hanging uselessly at my sides.

"All I wanted was a stone. If she could not get it for me for whatever reason, her soul would become mine. She wasn't even willing to ask for an extension of time. She just... gave up. Sad, really. I had such high hopes for her."

A stone?

My head perked up. If all it took was a stone, why wouldn't Jana just get it for him? Why hadn't she asked me for help? I wouldn't have let this happen to her. I would have given anything to save her, and I would have stopped at nothing to get it for her. Now-- she was dead.

Oh, God, my sister was *dead*.

The siekewa moved closer, as though my pain was a magnet. He stepped in Jana's blood, but didn't leave any footprints.

The bottle in his hand was glowing. Jana was in there, trapped forever because of her own stupidity. Why would she do something like that? Was it really so important to be more powerful? I shuddered, wrapping my arms around myself.

The siekewa was right in front of me now, and he took a step to the side, circling me. I didn't like it, but grief was starting to crush me, rooting my feet to the ground. All I could see were Jana's beautiful curls, stained red.

He was behind me, and I could smell a faint hint of ash clinging to him. His black robe brushed my bare ankle and I shuddered, finding my feet again and moving away from him. I was careful to avoid Jana's body as I stepped back towards the huge open glass doors.

There was a smile on his pale lips.

"You could save her, you know," he said seductively, promising hope.

"How?" I choked, ashamed that my voice broke in front of him. The only way I knew how to save a soul was to take its place, and as much as I loved Jana, I didn't know if I could do that.

"I just need a stone," he whispered, moving closer until he was in front of me again. He was taller than me, and I looked up, feeling my knees tremble.

"Why did Jana refuse to give it to you?" I demanded.

"I have absolutely no idea, although I'm sure she hadn't gotten it yet." He was nonchalant, but the words sounded hollow.

If I couldn't trade my soul for Jana's, I was going to figure out what she gave hers up for. "What stone?"

"If you can see me, then you can see the soul collectors. Each carries a stone that looks like an opal, but it glows with a fierce inner light. It is a badge, a symbol, nothing more. But I like shiny things, and I want one."

"Jana was going to steal one for you?" I asked, goosebumps lifting the hair on my arms.

"Yes. I want one of those stones. If you bring it to me, I will let your sister go."

"And if I can't do it?" I asked, my stomach rolling. I was thinking about making a deal with a siekewa. No matter how good it seemed, there was always a catch. There had to be.

"Then I keep her. I need souls to feed my powers. Without them, I can't grant wishes," he said, shrugging. "I will keep your sister until she is too tired to do anything more, and then I will set her free."

He'd set her free, but no collector would come to bring her to the afterlife. She would be stuck in this reality, quietly haunting the living.

It was cruel.

I had to save her. If I didn't, he would suck the magic out of her to keep going, to trick others into doing his bidding. If I could get a stone--and I knew the exact stone he was talking about--then I could free my sister. Of course, he had to have a better reason than a stone being pretty; he wanted it for something more, probably something bad, and I couldn't get him one if it meant worse than losing Jana.

I opened my mouth to say no way, but what came out was, "No time limits. I can back out at any time with no repercussions."

"None against you directly. Your sister, though, is mine until you get me that stone."

I hesitated, wondering if I could ever wash the dirt off my hands after this.

"You don't take my soul, ever," I countered, real fear rising in my chest.

"I will not take your soul unless you give it to me directly," he replied, stepping forward.

8

"I'll do it then," I said, proud that my voice didn't tremble. "I will get you your stone and then you will free my sister."

He snapped his fingers and another scroll appeared in the air. It unfurled in front of me, letters glittering in the dim lamp light. I read the words, making sure he hadn't added anything. I even checked the corners and the back for fine print.

He held out a pen, and when I took it, I felt an uncomfortable tingling in my fingers. The moment I started to write my name, it turned into pain. I remembered Jana's contract, and how it was signed in blood.

Disgusted, I signed the contract and threw the pen back at the siekewa. My name glistened on the scroll still hanging in the air before me: *Ellie Alwood.*

He caught it, and the contract disappeared with another snap of his fingers. I crossed my arms, wanting him to leave so I could break down into my hysterics and somehow manage to call the police.

Instead, he stepped even closer. The smell of ash made my nose tickle,and I glared up at him, even though my knees were trembling and I was starting to feel dizzy.

"There is only one thing left then," he whispered, his voice going low and husky.

I didn't like it and I certainly didn't trust it.

"I signed your contract. Our deal is done," I snapped, not liking that I could feel his breath tickling my face.

"Really, Ellie, you'd think you'd never dealt with a siekewa before." His smile was full of delight, and I stiffened when he cupped my face in his hands, the feel of his ruby ring cold on my cheek.

I could feel power through his icy skin. It

whispered so seductively that I gasped as it brushed against me.

And then he kissed me, his lips cold against my warm skin. I didn't try to pull away, realizing what he had meant. The Siekewa's Kiss was to seal the deal. It twined my fate to his, forming an unbreakable bond, so that whenever I was ready to pay my debt, all I would have to do was say his name.

The power that he held left his lips and filled my entire body with strength and purpose. Strong magic hummed through me, awakening all my senses. The world was painful for a moment, too vivid and alive, and then he pulled away.

His hands left my face at the same moment, and I collapsed to my knees, a sob escaping my lips. The power was gone, severed so quickly that I felt like a stranger in my own body.

He brushed a hand through my hair, and then he was gone, vanishing from the room with a soft pop.

I continued to sob, hugging and rocking myself. My sister was dead and I had made a deal with her killer. I was going to steal from the collectors to free Jana's soul.

And now I knew the monster's name: Drekvic.

CHAPTER TWO

The snow crunched underneath my feet as I stepped toward the dark casket. My eyes burned with unshed tears and I was certain my lower lip was starting to tremble, but I didn't break down when I put the white rose with the other flowers, and stepped back.

My mother, Kathy, followed, but she paused to kiss the smooth wood. I met her eyes when she turned to face me. Her gray eyes matched mine, but Jana had taken after her far more than I had. Her blonde hair was hidden under a black knit cap, and her round face was red from cold and crying. She was shorter than me and slid underneath my arm as I hugged her, slipping an arm around my waist as we watched the rest of Jana's friends pay their respects.

I stopped studying the people and started looking at the large cemetery hidden in snow. There were scattered trees and a few small hills, but mostly just graves.

I noticed a figure standing under one of the trees and I tensed. He had black hair and pale skin. I couldn't tell what color his eyes were, but I'd recognize the smug look on his face anywhere.

"What's wrong?" my mom asked. Even in her grief, she'd sensed the change in my mood.

I didn't want to worry her, so I just shook my head.

"It's nothing. I just want to go home."

"Me, too," she said.

I gave her a weak smile and glanced back at the tree. Drekvic was gone, but I still felt uneasy as the priest started lowering Jana's body into the ground.

We were the last to leave. Mom kept her arm around me, and I didn't let her go. My eyes were dry, but my chest felt heavy, and my nose wouldn't stop running.

"We should go," she said, giving me a quick squeeze before letting go.

We tromped back through the snow to our car. She had driven; her four-wheel drive handled better in the snow than my small electric car.

Her hands shook as she tried to unlock the door, so I took the keys from her. She gratefully climbed into the passenger seat.

It was a relief to be behind the wheel. I could focus on driving instead of the empty ache in my chest. I took my gloves off and turned on the heat, checking to make sure my mom was buckled safely in her seat. She closed her eyes and had tears running down her cheeks.

"I don't know what to do, Ellie," she whispered. "It's not supposed to be like this." Her voice broke, and she drew in a shaky breath.

My chest tightened, but I looked away, putting the vehicle in gear and turning the wheel to pull out of the parking spot.

"We'll figure it out," I said, making an effort to keep my voice even.

"When you two were little, I used to tell your

father that you would be the death of me. All the fights at school…" her voice trailed off, and she wiped her face. "You were always the trouble-maker. I never worried about Jana…"

"I'm sorry. I didn't protect her," I whispered, blinking back tears as I turned out onto the main road from the cemetery.

"Oh, Ellie." She reached for me, putting a hand on my leg and squeezing. "I didn't mean that. You always took care of her and always protected her. We both missed the signs."

I clenched my jaw, trying to keep my face stoic. I'd never lied to my mother before, and I hated that I was doing it now. She thought Jana committed suicide. In a way, she had, but it was because of a bad choice she'd made previously, a contract that she never should have signed. I stopped at a red light, closed my eyes for a moment and took a deep breath. I'd figure it out. I had to save Jana's soul, no matter what.

I drove us to my mother's home, sitting in silence while she tried to mask her muffled cries.

My keys were loud when I dropped them in the bowl by the door. The house smelled like cleaning solution and the fake lemon smell meant to cover it up. I had asked them to replace the beige carpet with hardwood floors, and the cold wood was unfamiliar to me.

With my coat and boots set out to dry, I turned into my office on the ground floor, passing several bookshelves along the way.

This was where I spent most of my free time, grading papers and working on lesson plans. It was also where I did research for my experiments. I still hadn't given up on finding a cure for addiction. My father was dead and didn't need it anymore, but there were other people out there that could use it.

I ran my fingers along the wooden work table that dominated the center of the room. My journal was open, my notes written in a neat and precise hand. I had been working with interlace patterns, building them with magic into a person's psyche, particularly their addictions, and then unraveling them, hopefully taking their illness with them.

So far all I'd managed to do was strip away pieces of personality, and I needed to refine the technique to be more precise about the molecules bound by it. I was trying to do that with different colors, but so far hadn't found the right ones.

I folded the large, hand-drawn diagrams and tucked them into the journal, dropped all my loose pens and markers into the recessed cup and placed the closed journal next to it, freeing up the majority of the space.

It looked empty, but I had a new project that took priority.

I had several clean journals, so I took one down and opened it up to the first page and wrote: *Getting a Stone*. I didn't sit when I worked, not liking the enclosed feel of it. Ideas needed space to grow and to move, so did my body if I wanted to have any ideas at all.

The first thing I needed to do was research. I knew the guides existed in multiple planes. They couldn't come to the first reality, so I had to find a way to reach out to theirs. If they were collecting souls, they would be behind just one gate, and one gate couldn't be *that* hard to get through.

The problem would be finding out what the stones did. I didn't know what their purpose was or how dangerous it would be to give one to Drekvic. I started pacing, holding my journal in my left hand as I tapped the pages with my pen.

I was pacing back and forth across the room when I turned and yelped, dropping the journal and jumping backwards.

Drekvic stood next to my table, looking through my old research book and frowning. He looked up at my startled noise and grinned.

"Hard at work?" he asked, laughing at me.

"What are you doing here?" I snapped, taking deep breaths to calm my racing heart.

"I was at the funeral. You didn't say anything to me, so I came to make sure you were alright," he said, putting the book down and taking a step toward me.

I bristled, almost snarling at him. "Get out." With jerky movements I scooped the journal and pen up off the floor, folding them against my chest.

"I just wanted to help," he said, shrugging.

I stomped past him, walking to the small desk by the window and slamming the journal on the table next to my laptop. I turned it on, trying to ignore the prickling power against the back of my neck. I didn't think he was here to hurt me, but all the hair on my arms was standing on end at his nearness.

"I have work to do. Leave."

I hit the keys harder than necessary as I forced out my password. The computer gave a happy little chirp and turned on.

"I just came to give you advice. I think you'll want to listen to what I have to say."

His voice was right in my ear, and I whirled around to face him. I had to look up, his pale face so close to mine.

"It's not worth whatever price you're selling it

for," I growled. I wanted to cross my arms, but he was close enough that I'd end up touching him, and that was never going to happen.

"It's free." He grinned, showing me his perfectly white teeth.

I just glared at him, refusing to speak. I hoped he couldn't hear my heart pounding or tell that my fisted hands were sweating despite the chilly weather.

"You're impossible," he mumbled, putting his hands on my shoulders and pushing me to the side.

I stumbled, catching myself before I ran into the nearest bookshelf and straightened, pulling on my magic. I was ready to fight, but all he did was sit down in my computer chair and start tapping on the keyboard.

"Look at this one and this one," he said after opening up two web browser windows. He gave me an impish grin and gestured to the black and red blog entry.

"This one is about me."

"I'm working here," I snapped. "Just get out."

He gave a melodramatic sigh and stood up. I didn't back up as he stepped closer to me. I wanted to strangle him, but I did nothing as he tipped my chin up with the knuckle on his right hand.

"I can't wait until I see you again," he said, his voice low.

It sent tingles up my spine, and I felt queasy. His lips were warm and dry as he kissed me my jaw, then vanished with a puff of smoke. I sneezed, reaching for my tissues as a second one built in my nose.

By the time they had passed, I took a deep breath, feeling it tremble in my chest. I sat down heavily, propping my elbows on the desk and covering my face with my hands. There was a lump in my throat making it difficult for me to breathe. I kept seeing Jana as she was when we were in school, young and happy, juxtaposed with the image of her lying dead on the floor.

I took a deep, shaky breath that sounded more like a sob and put my hands flat on the desk. I slowly counted to five, allowing myself only that long to compose my emotions.

The website Drekvic opened was a blog by a nature witch, and judging from the color scheme and title, I assumed it dealt with death magic. The title of the entry he'd opened was *Deal for Love*, and it was about a siekewa prince looking for a lover. Drekvic had said it was about him, but I didn't believe anything I was reading.

She claimed to have met Drekvic and read his tarot cards, trading the service for a lock of hair used in the reading. The cards had pointed him toward the future and said he would soon meet his true love.

I rolled my eyes, thinking it was a load of garbage and not at all helpful.

The other website was a little more promising. It was run by a store called "Gypsy Melo's Magical Shop." The name was familiar, so I opened another tab and checked the forum that I usually frequented to see if there were any comments on the shop.

I found one that mentioned she was extremely magical and knowledgeable, but had a habit of scamming her customers. Her shop had some top-notch items, but also had multiple Books of Shadows.

I frowned. Spell books weren't meant to be shared. Each spell was only a guideline and had to be adapted to work within the caster's limits and skills. Sharing a fully-formed spell, even if it worked for multiple people, could be dangerous, and it seemed Melo had her fair share of danger.

She had changed her name twice and this was her fourth shop in the area. I wondered how she kept getting a business license if she had so many charges against her.

Normally I wouldn't look twice at a resource like this, but Drekvic had left it there specifically for me. I didn't trust him, but if he wanted this stone, he wouldn't do something to hinder my progress.

I settled in and started to read.

CHAPTER THREE

The first time I saw him, I was helping a group of elderly women draw Celtic knots. I knew he wasn't here for one of the other souls in the room, but I couldn't say why that I knew that. He was pretending not to study me, but his attention felt like fire upon my skin. I looked up suddenly, catching his brown eyes, but he glossed over me, once again, looking at everyone in the room but me.

I didn't avert my gaze, determined to know who he was and what he wanted. The collector's weren't supposed to really interact with the living, and as I was clearly actively alive, he shouldn't be shadowing me. I worried he'd somehow figured out my deal with Drekvic, but I hadn't told anyone or even spoken the words aloud. I didn't think that Drekvic would tell the collectors that I was trying to steal from them, so who was he? He never looked at me again, and my attention was distracted by an elderly woman that asked me to help her find the perfect shade of green for her apple.

My decision to volunteer at the nursing home helped me fulfill two desperate needs. The first was to get out of the empty house. I had cashed in all my vacation and bereavement hours to take time off teaching at the college, and had been spending all my days locked in my office researching, and I needed a break. The second was to find the soul guides. They liked to gather in places where death was common, especially death that people could see coming.

Even if they were welcome in these spaces, I didn't like seeing them quietly courting the souls of the dying. Was that why the strange collector was looking at me? Was I dying? I didn't like the idea of that, but I looked up at him again anyways. He glanced away again, his strong jaw clenching slightly.

I stood up, excusing myself from the table. His body shifted slightly, his lean muscles tensing as I moved forward. I tried not to look at him as I walked to his corner. He was tall, looming over me by at least six inches. His black hair was messy and fell around his face and into his eyes. His ivory skin was perfect, with no scars or freckles marring it. His opal stone was tight against his neck, and I tried to keep my gaze anywhere but on the side of the room where he stood.

Finally, I was close enough that I could see him studying me out of the corner of my eye. I was close enough that if he'd been in our reality, it wouldn't have been weird for me to talk to him or greet him. The hair on my arms stood up as I gathered my nerves. Swiftly, I turned and faced him. He was gone.

Frustrated, I went back to my table, trying to ignore the other soul collectors that I passed. They were quietly talking to the living, their voices unheard for now. They were a colorful bunch, each collector having made the choice to give up their afterlife and any future lives in order to live forever. Their payment for immortality was to become the guides of souls, taking them through the seven gates of the afterlife.

The collectors could come from any type of background and any type of moral fiber, but the choice to live forever was a binding one, and I'd never heard of any collector retiring.

Still, they all looked content with their lot, and the glowing stones were on their necks. Tears threatened to overwhelm me. How was I supposed to save Jana if I couldn't even get close enough to the collectors to talk to them, much less steal a stone from them? I had to try something different. Every day I took to figure it out was a day Jana spent in captivity and torture. I needed to save her. I was running out of options.

* * *

After a week of online research and dead ends with more reputable sources, and a weekend of volunteer work, I had no new leads. I finally found myself driving down a narrow street just after eleven in the morning, listening to my GPS tell me to keep going straight.

Even this early, there were people lounging on the street corners. Some looked like gang members, with white undershirts that clung to their gaunt forms. There were women, too, wearing mini-dresses and high heels with too much make up. I stood out like a man in a bra store, my clothes revealing nothing but my face and hands. It was still cold outside. They had to be wearing heat charms or they'd freeze.

I adjusted my grip on the steering wheel, not liking the way some of their eyes followed my car. My vehicle wasn't high-end, but it was newer than every car I passed. It was hard not to feel self-conscious, even if I'd done nothing wrong. Being out here was enough for some people, and I didn't want to draw their attention, even if I was confident enough in my skills that none of them would be able to seriously hurt me.

I saw the sign before my GPS told me I'd arrived. "Gypsy Melo's Magical Shop" was one dingy storefront in a street of dingy storefronts, but her neon sign stuck out from all the faded plastic.

The parking lot across the street was relatively empty, so I pulled in and found a space close to the sidewalk. I looked around before climbing out of my car, clutching my white purse tight against my chest as I quickly locked the door. I started walking toward a crosswalk, stepping around the trash that collected on the curb that distinguished the parking lot from the walkway. Old newspapers were frozen into the cement, and I avoided those patches, too, not wanting to slip.

I checked both ways before crossing the street and avoided eyes of the sex worker on the corner. I could sense her staring at me, but she didn't approach and didn't talk to me, and it made me feel a little bit better.

I ran my thumb across the inside of my sapphire ring, drawing comfort from the fact that I had enough magic to protect myself. Every night I set a small circle to push any excess energy into the ring, and I hadn't cast any major spells since Jana died that would have drained the magic. Being prepared was one of the few things I did to excess.

Melo's shop was two doors from the corner. It was shabby, with red paint peeling off the door and windows fogged over with age. The chipped sign was black with red letters and neon pink around the edges.

I hesitated, staring at the brass handle. Melo's blog had been extremely detailed in collector's lore. Based on her observations, I was fairly certain that she could see them just like I could. She mentioned the stone that they all carried and called it a soul. I didn't understand how a stone could be a soul, but I felt confident from her writing that she knew more about them than I did.

The metal was cold through my gloves as I pulled open the door and went inside.

The shop was hushed after the ambient noise from the street. It smelled of dust and old leather, and a bell tinkled as the door shut behind me. I turned in a half circle, admiring the large collection in front of me.

The merchandise was lined up in several free-standing shelves, open on both sides so I could see through the shop to the back wall. There were all types of magical paraphernalia, from all different disciplines.

The dried herbs were for nature witches, along with several rows of seeds in case they wanted to start their own gardens. The religious symbols took up two entire bookcases, ranging from Celtic knots to crucifixes and ancient symbols from Greece and Norway. The most packed shelves were piled with hundreds of old books. Most were leather-bound, and from where I was standing I could see that they didn't have the traditional titles on the spines. These were spell books, and I could feel the magic radiating off them from the door.

I was slightly disappointed to see them, but I understood the sentiment. Knowledge was important, and techniques that might work for one witch could work for another. The problem was that not everyone was careful--they could end up killing themselves... or others.

Movement from the counter caught my attention, and I looked back toward the far side of the shop. There was a lit glass case full of precious stones, like my sapphire, meant for gathering power.

It was the woman behind the counter that had drawn my eye, as she walked into the front room from the beaded doorway behind her. She fluffed her silver curls and adjusted her black apron over a dark red dress. She seemed surprised when she looked up to see me, her wrinkles making deep furrows on her face. Her eyes were a beautiful gold with a hint of green around the pupil. It was a color that I would expect to see on a lion. Melo wasn't a witch, like I had originally thought. She was a shape-shifter.

"Good afternoon," she said, her voice carrying a faint Italian accent. "How can I help you today?"

"I'm looking for Melo," I replied, holding my bag close while trying to look confident.

"That would be me. And you are?"

"I'm Ellie," I said, not extending my hand. I didn't quite trust this woman, as some of her blog entries hinted at dark magic and loose morals. At the moment, I reminded myself, she was all I had.

"I was sorry to hear about your sister," Melo said, folding her slender fingers across each other on the counter.

Slightly taken aback, I looked away. Tears stung my eyes, but I blinked them back. I was going to save Jana's soul. I didn't have time to grieve, and I didn't want to show weakness in front of this shifter.

"Thank you. Did you know Jana?" I asked, proud my voice didn't break.

"Oh yes," Melo said. "She liked to come in on the weekends and listen to my stories. I went to the funeral, but I didn't introduce myself. Most people like to pretend that my kind doesn't exist, so it was easy enough to fade into the background."

I nodded, not really knowing what to say. Shape-shifters used to be hunted for their magical properties. Their bones, skin, and hair could be used for the most powerful of nature spells. The fact that they were sentient didn't seem to bother my witching ancestors. It was only a couple hundred years ago that the shifters chose to curse their own bodies and the bodies of their children to be left alone. Anyone that killed a shifter for their body parts would find themselves plagued with one hundred years of bad luck. Some nature witches scoffed at that--until their children were kidnapped or their house burned down. The shifters were no longer hunted, and they were finally able to get laws passed that made it illegal to hurt them.

Still, shape-shifters and witches just didn't like each other. I understood why, but I didn't feel it myself. Killing someone with a soul was wrong, no matter how magical their bodies.

"I wish you would have," I said, unable to help myself. "I would have liked to know more of Jana's friends. I—I didn't recognize anyone aside from family."

Melo nodded and stood up straighter, rocking back and forth on her heels. She looked ready to flee.

"Since you didn't recognize me, I take it that this isn't a social call." She raised an eyebrow, waiting expectantly.

Feeling awkward, I walked closer to the counter, trying not to fidget with the zippers on my purse. "I read your blog, and I thought… I thought that maybe you're like me."

"Like you? How?" Her voice was wary, and I wondered if she had bad experiences with people reading her blog and visiting her shop.

"I can see the spirit guides," I whispered, feeling odd as I said it out loud. I hadn't told anyone since middle school, when the other girls in my class wouldn't believe me.

"I know you can," Melo sighed, running a hand through her hair to make the curls fluff up. "Your sister told me. That was why she came to me originally. She wanted to see them, too."

"I need to go to the spirit plane," I blurted; the talk of Jana just reminded me that she was gone.

"And why would you need to do that?" Her voice was terse. She didn't seem annoyed, but... scared, maybe?

I didn't know what to tell her. To say that Jana had made a deal with the siekewa was almost as bad as saying that I had done it myself, even if my reasons were only to protect her. Seeing my silence, all the color drained from Melo's face.

"She made a deal with him, didn't she?" she gasped, reaching out behind her to grab at a stool. She sat down on it, looking pale and a hundred years older.

"How do you know about him?" I demanded, all nerves gone as I leaned aggressively on the counter. "Did you tell her how to summon him?"

"She found out about it here, but no, I never taught her how to summon him. There's a customer that comes in every couple weeks to buy religious artifacts. He told Jana once that the siekewas would grant any wish as long... as long as you can pay the price."

Melo glanced at me, sadness in her eyes. I didn't like it, and what she said next made me feel worse.

"Jana wanted to be like you. She said you always knew where you were going, always had a plan. She thought it stemmed from you being able to see the edges of the spirit world... and she was envious. When I told her it was something you were born with and not a skill that could be taught, she began

26

exploring other options."

I shuddered and turned away. Drekvic had implied that very same thing. I didn't understand why, but apparently Jana wanted to be more like me. Her bright spirit and easy-going manner weren't enough for her, and she had felt like I overshadowed her? I bit back tears, unwilling to cry in front of a woman I'd just met.

When I turned around, it was with my chin held high.

"I need to get to the spirit world to save her soul."

"If the siekewa has it, the only way to save it would be to make a deal with him."

I nodded. "I already have."

Melo studied me, her eyes almost glowing in the dim light. I clenched my jaw, and stared back at her unflinchingly. I could sense her testing the air with her magic, just a gentle nudge to see if Drekvic had followed me into her store.

After what felt like forever she blinked, breaking eye contact and nodded.

"Then I'll help you, but you're both idiots for trusting a siekewa. They never lie, but they rarely tell the whole truth either." Melo reached for a latch behind the counter and swung it to the side, gesturing for me to join her behind it.

"I know," I mumbled, frustrated at being treated like a child.

"Then you made the wrong choice," she admonished, but didn't close the latch until after I'd passed her.

CHAPTER FOUR

The back room of Melo's shop was quiet. She had flipped the "Open" sign to "Closed" in the front window to avoid interruptions, leaving me to sit alone on a big leather chair to wait, while she went downstairs for something that was supposed to help me traverse planes.

I studied my surroundings, noticing how worn the wooden floors were. I could tell where people walked the most, an indented groove from the front door to the shelves lining the walls.

There were more spell books back here, but also more dried herbs and flowers. I noticed a locked cabinet in the farthest corner, almost hidden in the shadow of a shelf. There were two cast iron padlocks keeping it shut, and I worried what might be in there.

I pulled a small charm from my purse. It was a glass marble, completely clear except for a pinprick of blue in the center. The color matched my sapphire and the color of my magic, making it easier for me to use the object for spells. This one was meant to check the ambient energy of a room, and when I sent a small sliver of power into the marble, it glowed a pale blue.

I put it away, feeling better. If there was anything

malicious in the room, the marble would have turned violet, the red warning obscured by the blue of my magic.

I rubbed the back of my neck, still not liking the idea of being in the shop alone with the woman. For all her honesty, I had only just met Melo, and it would have been stupid to trust her so blindly. I hadn't even told anyone where I was going, too ashamed to say I was meeting a crazy lady in the bad part of town to find a way into the spirit world to save my sister's soul.

I sighed, leaning forward to rest my elbows on my knees and bury my face in my hands. Before, my biggest worry was whether or not my students were learning anything, and now I was off to rescue my fool of a sister.

I was so mad at her I almost wanted to let her rot. She had made a deal with a monster so that she could see the collectors. She thought that was something special. And if she could see them after he granted her wish, why hadn't she told me? We could have talked about it. I'd wanted someone else to share that experience with for so long... it would have meant the world to me to know that Jana could see them too.

I could hear Melo's heavy footsteps clomping up the stairs. I jerked upright, not wanting to show my emotions. The stronger she thought I was, the better. I didn't want her to change her mind because she thought I was too much of a baby.

The older woman reached the top of the stairs, and I was surprised to see her carrying one of the very stones I was trying to get. It looked different, but recognizable. The glow wasn't as bright and the colors inside seemed faded. It had to be a fake. I wanted to ask her about it, but I figured that she would tell me eventually.

Melo pulled up a wooden chair with a large cushion. It didn't look as comfortable as the couch, but she plopped down and sighed with contentment.

"Going up and down those stairs is hard on my old bones," she mumbled, leaning forward over the coffee table. She pushed several piles of paper and stacks of magazines to the side, and I winced as some fell on the floor. She didn't seem concerned about it as she set the stone down in the empty space, balancing it until it was still.

She took a piece of chalk from her apron pocket and drew a circle around the stone. She kept drawing a spiral. As I watched, the stone seemed to change color, from cool white to a pale blue. The closer she got to the center, the darker the color became until I could almost hear it buzzing.

Finally, when the chalk touched the stone, Melo pulled back and the gem was a deep midnight-blue, so dark it almost looked black.

"What is it?" I asked, unable to help myself.

I'd never seen a shape-shifter do magic. They were more likely to perform religious magic than the traditional spirit magic that I was classically trained in. Religious magic was only as powerful as the practitioner's belief. If they waivered, the magic could easily backfire, which was why most witches tended to stay away from it if they could.

"It's a replica of the stones the guides wear," Melo replied, sitting back with a look of satisfaction. "It's not as good as the real thing, and it wouldn't fool one of them, but it will make your crossing easier."

I looked at her, brow furrowed.

"The stones help the souls and guides cross between planes. This stone only works one way. It will help you get there, but you'll have to find a way back on your own."

I started picking imaginary dirt from under my nails. What if I was stuck in the spirit world? When I died, would my collector be able to find me or would I end up stuck in limbo like the ghosts I sometimes saw?

"You don't have to do this," Melo said. "I have never tried, though I've had this stone for years."

I thought of Jana's soul being used as a siekewa's power source, sucked dry until she was so washed up not even a collector could find her signature to bring her home.

"I have to," I whispered, feeling light-headed.

"Then give me your hand," she said, nodding in understanding.

I held it out and she took it. Her skin was warm, and I could feel the life humming through her. I learned a lot about Melo with that one touch, although I tried not to let it seep too far into me. Whenever I met someone new, I could sense who they were and how long they had lived with a single touch. It was my special brand of magic.

She was over a hundred years old, probably closer to two-hundred. I knew that she had spent a large part of her life as an animal rather than dealing with human politics. She was stronger in her magic than I'd originally thought, and her warmth and feeling for Jana was spilling over into her thoughts for me. I could feel her apprehension at giving me the means to go to the spirit world, but her confidence that it would work was reassuring.

I saw Melo's eyes soften, and I realized that she could feel it too. My eyes opened wider and I looked up at her, wonder pushing out every other feeling.

"You're just like me," I whispered.

"When you come home to this reality, you are welcome here anytime," Melo replied, a smile making her weathered face seem beautiful. "I know how hard it is to feel alone."

"Thank you."

And that was the last thing I said before she pushed my open palm down onto the stone.

The world spun and I felt like I was falling. The power that raced through me was warm and comforting, but it hurt as it pulled my body from the hard physics of reality and into the open chaos of the spirit world. Everything started to prickle with energy and light, and it was starting to heat up my skin.

I could no longer sense Melo next to me, or feel her hand pushing mine down into the stone. The leather chair was long gone, and with a rush of cold air that felt like ice against me, I was dropped unceremoniously onto the ground.

I tasted dirt in my mouth and grass tickled my nose. The air was cold, but comfortable. The magic that had been rushing through me was gone, and my body felt like lead. I couldn't get my hands underneath me, and I wasn't sure how I was going to sit up.

That problem was solved for me, as a pair of rough hands jerked me upright. The world spun again and the light hurt my eyes. I blinked rapidly, trying to make my legs work. I tried to raise my hands to push away from whoever was touching me, but they hit uselessly against black leather.

Finally, I was able to focus on the person holding me up by my ruined gray shirt. It was the collector that had been watching me, and the intensity of his gaze took my breath away.

He was wearing a leather vest with silver buckles

over a dark green t-shirt that hugged his chest and arms. I'd never seen a man wearing leather pants, but I decided that they fit this particular man very well. His boots were black leather as well, and the stylized vine tattoo curling around his right arm completed the bad-boy biker look.

I felt my face flush as I scrambled to find my feet, so I requested a hint of power from my sapphire ring. The magic burned through me, crisp and clean, pushing away the last of the weakness, and I was able to stand on my own.

I pushed against his chest, trying not to think of how his muscles were bunched from trying to hold me up. He didn't let go of my shirt, still evaluating me with his dark eyes. I stared back at him, frowning with displeasure at being man-handled.

"Let go," I demanded, grabbing his wrists. His skin was warm, and I felt a tingle of power in him. What I didn't feel though, was the rush of his past that I always felt when meeting someone new. It was disorienting, and, for a moment, my confusion won out over irritation that he was stretching my clothes.

"You're not dead," he replied, his dark eyes as confused as mine.

"No, I'm not," I snapped.

"I was following you because I was told that you would need to be collected, but this must be Fate's idea of a joke." His voice was irritated, but even so, it was beautiful. It was a gentle tenor, and I felt the cadence of it tingle all the way down my spine.

I shook my head, trying not to let his musical voice get to me as I thought about what I needed to do.

I saw his stone, nestled against the hollow of his throat, held by a black string. It was tight against his neck, like a choker. The stone was glowing slightly, faint rose colors swirling within the whiteness of the rock. I could practically feel the power humming off of it. Melo was right, hers was a cheap imitation.

"What in Fate's name am I supposed to do with you?" he sighed, releasing me and turning away.

I took a step back, glad to have space between us.

He was pushed to the back of my mind as I was able to take in our surroundings.

We were standing in a world I thought only existed in paintings. The grass was a vibrant green, spotted with small wildflowers that ranged from pink to pale blue. The forest beyond the small meadow seemed to beckon to me, with its colorful birds and innocent animals roaming along its grassy edge. On the meadow's other side was a sparkling beach surrounding a glistening lake. The water was so clear I could see fish swimming in its depths. There was a wooden dock that went out into the water and a small wooden rowboat tied up to it.

I took a step towards the water, still lost in awe, but the collector cleared his throat, clearly annoyed that I was ignoring him.

I blushed again, feeling like a school girl, and turned towards him with my arms crossed.

"Well, Miss Alwood, I think it is important that all souls know their guides. My name is Chester Sandsil. Since you're not dead, I cannot take you to the after-life, and since there is no place for you here in this reality, I recommend you find it in your heart to make your way back to yours." He crossed his arms sourly.

"I'm not leaving," I replied. "I have a mission here, and I'm going to complete it."

"You have a mission?" he asked, incredulous.

"I don't see how that's any of your business," I replied, turning firmly away from him and heading toward the beach. Chester followed.

"Let's hurry and get it done, so you can be off to do whatever you need to do, and I can get a *real* assignment." He was clearly annoyed.

"None of your business," I repeated back over my shoulder.

I couldn't tell him I was going to steal a spirit guide's stone for a siekewa to save my sister's soul. As little information I had about the collectors, I knew that probably wouldn't go over well.

I stayed silent on my walk to the beach. I wasn't sure what I was going to accomplish there, but I had decided I wanted a better look at the water, and perhaps more time to think about what I was going to tell him. I reached the sand and crunched across it, glad that it was firm and I didn't sink in and ruin my shoes.

I could feel the magic rolling off Chester like heat waves. He didn't make a noise that I could hear, and it was unnerving to know he was so close despite my footsteps being the only sounds.

I stopped when I got to the edge of the dock and looked down into the water.

"It's my business," Chester growled into my ear, startling me, "because while you are in the spirit world, I am supposed to be your guide. Since you're not dead, I can't take you beyond, so you're stuck with me until you leave."

I turned to face him, trying to muster my best glare, but instead found myself looking at his chin. I had to look up, angling my face so my brows made it look like I was glaring.

"I am here to save my sister," I replied, not wanting to tell him that she had sold her soul for power.

He sighed, running a hand over his face. He

whispered something to himself that sounded suspiciously like "foolish mortals." I straightened my back and waited, lifting my chin up so I was looking down my nose, even though he was taller than me.

"You can't save your sister if she's a ghost. She is lost to the in-between," he explained, shaking his head and putting his hands on his trim hips.

"I will do whatever I have to do to save her," I replied.

"Have you ever seen a ghost?" he demanded, looking like he wanted to throttle me.

"Actually, I have." I turned away from him, looking out over the waves to the far side of the lake. There were mountains in that direction covered in dark green woods.

"Then you know that they can't be reasoned with. You can't pull them from the spirit world because they won't go. They are called lost for a reason."

"My sister isn't like that."

He threw up his hands in disgust and stalked away from me down the dock. He still made no noise, even though the deck was creaking with age.

"You're going to get yourself killed," he muttered.

I put my hands on my own hips and glared back at him, satisfied that he wouldn't try to stop me. My confidence wavered when the look of irritation on his face turned to concern.

I hadn't noticed the sun's warmth until it was gone, and from behind me there was a cool dampness that tickled the back of my neck.

I turned around to see the monster's rows of teeth grinning down at me.

"Oh crap."

CHAPTER FIVE

The monster was swan-like, its slender neck curved elegantly as it tilted its blue-skinned face to look at me. Its pointy teeth were longer than my arms, and as thick as my torso. It was huge, looking over me and blocking out the sun. I caught my reflection in the black depths of the one eye I could see, and I looked terrified.

The color of its pebbly skin shifted with the light, casting a perfect reflection of the world around it, making it easy to sneak up on prey. I had a hard time finding its edges even though I could see its teeth quite clearly.

Gaping like an idiot, I dropped to the wooden dock right as the creature turned its head to snap its jaws shut where I had just been standing. The damn thing was sentient, and it had used magic to bespell me. I was too far from the shore; I wasn't getting out of this.

The creature made a high-pitched squeal of frustration that sounded very wrong coming from something so large. It leaned its head back, ready to strike again and perhaps take the entire end of the dock out with me.

I tried to scramble backwards, but I ran into

something solid and immovable. I looked up, panicked, and realized I'd forgotten Chester. He had a large sword in his grip glowing a bright green color. I couldn't tell what the weapon was made of, but he looked like he knew how to use it.

The hilt molded around his hand as though it were made for him alone. The glow from the blade made it impossible to read the writing I saw shimmering in the light. Even though the thing was almost as large as him, Chester held it up with only his right hand as though it weighed nothing. His muscles looked tense, but not straining like mine would have been. I wondered where the bloody thing had been a moment ago. It was too big for me to miss it.

The creature hissed, angrily. It was afraid of Chester, but it also wanted a snack. I shuddered to think that I was inches away from being fish food. I scooted around Chester until he was between the monster and me, not above sacrificing him to stay alive.

"She's under my protection, Tabitha," Chester growled, his voice dangerous.

I saw her first, the thing whispered, its voice echoing through my mind. I didn't like the slimy feel of it and immediately drew on my magic to wipe it from me.

"She is *mine*," Chester repeated, and I stared in surprise as his hair started to float as he drew upon his magic. His entire face took on a different light, as though he was glowing from within. His dark eyes seemed to suck in the light and the green color from his sword flowed up his hands and wrists until his forearms were glistening completely with it.

I could feel Tabitha's disgust in my mind as she turned away and slunk underwater.

Chester turned towards me, his displeasure still radiating. The magic started to fade, and I noticed the sword disappearing as well. When he let go of the hilt, it faded in a wisp of smoke. The sword had been made of magic? I hadn't even known that was possible. When his skin finally stopped glowing, I dared a look at his face.

"Let's go," he ordered, holding his hand out.

I didn't want to take orders from him, but he had just saved my life… and I also realized that he could probably kill me without a second thought, so I begrudgingly put my hand in his. He pulled me to my feet and jerked me towards him. A burst of energy shot through me as his grip tightened to wrap around my shoulders. I tried to jerk away, but the world vanished and I couldn't breathe.

Everything was frozen. I lost all sense of time and space as the world spun in a kaleidoscope of color. The only thing that was real was Chester's steady green aura next to mine, his body burning against me where I held onto him for dear life. The cold was numbing my senses, and I started to feel like I was going to faint.

Then, we popped back into existence and I was me again. My knees buckled and I fell into him. Chester's arms were still steady around me, keeping me from falling on my face.

"Maybe a little warning next time," I warbled, surprised that I could speak at all.

He sighed and lifted me slightly so I could get my feet underneath me. He didn't let go of me until I wasn't swaying in place. I still felt like I could vomit, but I must not have looked like I was going to, because he stepped away from me and crossed his arms.

I took a deep breath and looked around. We were in a strange place that had to be a city, but it was like nothing I'd ever seen before. All the buildings looked like spun glass, delicate and fanciful. They seemed to change colors depending on what angle I was looking from, and their reflections on the ground when the light shone through were amazing. Despite looking clear and reflecting the sun, I couldn't see the inside of the buildings unless there was an opening or a window. The walkways were all made of the same multi-colored glass, and I knelt down to touch it.

When I tapped it with my knuckle it made a clear, ringing sound that reverberated in my chest.

There were flowers and trees made from the same crystal as well, blending seamlessly with the buildings. A gentle breeze lifted the loose hair off the back of my neck, and the leaves chimed together, making a chorus of music that gave me chills.

I'd never imagined that the spirit world could be so beautiful. From the glimpses of it that I had seen, it always looked dark and gray with nothing of worth. I was finding it to be the complete opposite, and I wanted to keep exploring.

"Are you finished?" Chester grumbled, interrupting my observations. He was glaring at me from under his eyebrows, clearly annoyed.

To be honest, I'd only really known him for all of twenty minutes, and he was annoyed for every single one of them. Maybe that was just his state of being. I shrugged him off and continued to look around.

There were collectors here, too. Their black necklaces and opal-like stones gave them away immediately. Without the stones, I would have thought they were just a rag-tag group of people. There was a young girl that looked like a fairy princess in a wispy green dress and delicate pink wings. I saw a bald man step out of a building, wearing a dark red robe that was so ornate it must have weighed at least fifty pounds. And then there was Chester, biker leather and all.

"Look, you can gawk more later. We need to move off the circle," Chester snarled, reaching out and grabbing my upper arm to pull us off the circular patch of sidewalk we had landed on.

I jerked away, but followed behind him anyways.

"They're landing pads. They're safer to land on, rather than accidentally appearing on top of someone. They need to be kept clear. If others come, we would be in their way," he explained, pointing at where we had appeared.

I noticed that there were symbols along the edge of the glass circle, but I didn't recognize the language.

"The collectors live here?" I asked, unable to contain the admiration in my voice.

"Yes. You can look while we walk," he said, gesturing for me to follow him along a path that led through the buildings.

I followed him, gawking as we went. I wasn't the only one. Whenever a collector noticed me, they stopped and stared back, slack-jawed. I looked away, unnerved by their wide eyes and open mouths. As we turned down a more crowded path, I decided to look down at my feet.

"Why can't they look somewhere else?" I mumbled, glancing away from another pair of shocked eyes.

"Your spirit is glowing with life. Collectors are drawn to it, along with all the other nasty creatures in the area." He glanced back at me, and I saw worry in his dark gaze. "If we don't get you back to your world,

I don't know how long we can keep your soul and your body together."

"I need to save my sister," I said, stubbornly. So far, I really hadn't come up with a plan to steal a stone. They were all on short necklaces and it would be really obvious if I tried to take one. Besides, with no way to get back to my world, I didn't have an exit plan.

"Yeah, yeah," Chester mumbled, waving a dismissive hand. "You can't save her. I told you that already."

I thought about running away. If they had a way to send me back, I needed to steal a stone before leaving, otherwise there'd be no point to this little adventure. Still... this place made me nervous. Tabitha had almost eaten me. If Chester hadn't been there... I wanted to shiver, but I forced my nerves down. I had to save Jana and this was the only way I knew how.

Not liking the corner I had gotten myself into, I followed Chester sullenly up the colorful walk to a large building. A grand design stretched out on either side of the door, looking like the actual wings of a bird with delicate carved feathers gracing the roof. Belatedly, I saw the center figure of the building was a woman, and we entered through a door in her stomach. The building was carved like an angel?

I didn't have time to contemplate, because Chester walked through the door with purposeful strides. He kept glancing back to make sure I was still there, but the tension in his shoulders kept me from dawdling. I hurried inside the propped open doors and entered the largest library I had ever seen in my life.

I stumbled to a stop, my mouth dropping open.

Unlike the cool crystal outside, the inside of the building was all warm browns and reds, stretching out to the left and right of me with fifteen-foot ceilings that were a pale cream color. The shelves of books were at least ten feet high and went all the way to the back wall, row upon row, to either side. In the center of the room was a large sitting area with chairs and large tables meant for research where people could also relax and read. Within the shelves I could see several nooks against circular windows that were also perfect places to read in natural light. The entire place was hushed and silent, permeated with knowledge so thick that I could almost feel it on my skin.

I wanted more time to explore the library, but my guide was rapidly disappearing through the sitting room toward the back offices. I hurried to catch up with him, glad that most of the collectors here had their noses in books and were not paying me any attention.

The only exception was a young man sitting on a window seat near the entrance. I only glanced at him, noting how brightly his pale blonde hair stood out against his dark skin as I side-stepped gracefully around the chairs and tables to catch up with Chester.

He had stopped in front of a sliding door and pressed a button with an arrow on it. I realized that we were waiting for an elevator, and the mundane action surprised me after all the splendor and magic of the last half hour. He glanced over to make sure that I was behind him, and I swear I saw the hint of a smile at the edge of his lips.

I crossed my arms and refused to acknowledge this sudden twist in his emotions. I could see that his shoulders had relaxed, too. The library seemed to be working its magic on his nerves also.

The elevator doors slid open with a pleasant chime and we stepped into the small space. I was thankful that it was just a normal elevator, with mirrored box walls and a plain, but pretty, tile floor. It was a tight fit for the both of us, and Chester's arm brushed my shoulder as it took us upward.

There were three floors in the building, and we went up to the top one. It was a short ride, but Chester's magic seemed to heat the tiny space. I was warm by the time the doors slid open, and I gratefully scrambled out. The room we entered into was comfortable. The walls and floor were covered in dark oak panels. There were low shelves all over the room that held several small statues and scrolls, protected from the elements by glass compartments. It looked more like a museum than an office.

On the far side of the room sat a woman looking out one of two oddly shaped windows. They were the eyes of the angel outside. I wanted to take a closer look, but Chester's steps were wary. I stopped only a few paces from the elevator.

The woman turned when Chester got to the edge of her plain wooden desk. She was easily the most stunning woman that I had ever seen. Her face was a perfect heart shape with an elegant jawline and a long neck. Her golden hair was in an elaborate braid that fell over one shoulder, accented by little stones that glinted with magic. They looked like the stones the collectors wore. Would such a small one satisfy Drekvic? He hadn't specified the size.

The woman smiled and her violet eyes lit up like stars in the night sky. "You found her, then?" she asked Chester, her voice sounding pure and clean. It echoed through the room like a brilliant bell.

"She's not dead," Chester replied, crossing his arms and trying to look annoyed. His shoulders were thrown back and his chin lifted slightly. It reminded

44

me of when I had to face my boss and knew that she wouldn't like what I was going to tell her.

"Of course she's not dead," the woman laughed.

She came around the desk and walked toward me. Her dress was a wispy blue color, accented with more of those stones. Against the fabric they looked like coral underwater.

"You have no idea how long I have waited for this meeting," she said softly as she approached me. I wanted to step back, but I was nearly pressed against the closed elevator doors already. There wasn't anywhere for me to go.

The woman wrapped her arms around me, the smile never leaving her face. Her cheek met mine, and my knees buckled.

The rush of her history crushed me like a leaf under her shoe. This woman was ancient. She hardly looked older than me, but she had memories from thousands of years ago. Those burned brightest, as though she had spent a lot of time thinking about them.

She was standing in front of the Egyptian Pyramids as they were being built, and then she was teaching a primitive kind of human to build a fire. The images kept flickering, and I felt sick to my stomach. When a wave of her magic washed over me, I lost all sense of time and space.

I could hear her laughing as she held me upright. I couldn't find my center in the huge ocean of energy that came with her touch. I had thought Drekvic's magic was powerful, but this woman... her magic was beyond compare. I was drowning, lost in space, alone.

I shuddered, feeling wetness on my cheeks, and heard a man's voice shouting angrily through the chaos.

A pair of arms grabbed my shoulders, pulling me away from the woman and back into him. Immediately her memories stopped flickering in my mind, and while I could still feel the enormity of her magic, I could also feel the minuscule smear that was mine. I lunged for it, pulling in deep gasps of air as I drew power from the sapphire ring sparking on my hand.

It wasn't until the last of the adrenaline finished coursing through me that I realized I was leaning completely on Chester for support. Flushing, I immediately scrambled to get my feet underneath me and pulled away. He released me without comment, glaring at the woman across from us both.

His hands hovered at his sides, like he was ready to grab me and shove me behind him if she tried to touch me again.

I wanted to kick myself. Two people in the past fortnight had managed to get me power drunk with just a single touch. I felt like a child trying to play football with giants. What had Jana gotten me into?

"I'm sorry, Ellie," the woman crooned, looking contrite. "I haven't met one of your kind in so long, I'd forgotten how sensitive you are to magic."

"You didn't forget," Chester muttered, but I wasn't sure if the woman heard him.

I wanted to ask what she meant by my kind, but I had other questions first. "Who are you?" I demanded, proud that my voice was firm and didn't betray the terror in my chest.

"It's just like Chester to bring you here without any warning of who you might encounter. I am Fate, one of the three gods that created the world."

If I hadn't been able to sense her history, I would have said that she was lying without a second thought. The gods didn't exist, at least, *I* had never believed in them. Even knowing how old she was, I still wasn't sure. Somehow seeing my thoughts, she smiled.

"You have doubts?" she asked.

"Maybe you're just really old," I said, careful to keep my voice emotionless. I felt ready to burst.

She laughed, hugging her stomach and bending over as though I had just told the world's funniest joke.

"Oh, Ellie, you know that's not true. You can read magic as easily as you can read history. Can you imagine anyone having more power than me?" she asked sweetly.

I grimaced. Power grew with age, and this creature was extremely old. It was hard to ignore, but I'd gone my entire life without faith.

"Just trust her," Chester said, his voice cracking slightly.

I wrinkled my nose at him, wondering why he thought I even trusted *him* much less his advice.

"If you don't, she'll try to prove it to you, and it hurts." He shrugged at my confused look, but I saw his throat move as he swallowed.

"I can give a demonstration," Fate taunted, grinning wickedly.

Her exposed teeth made me shiver and I shook my head.

"I believe you. You're a goddess."

"Liar," Fate laughed, moving forward. Chester tried to stop her, but she snatched my hand tightly before he could get in the way.

I flinched, but she didn't let go. Her power drowned me again, and I whimpered. I'd *never* had a second vision, but Fate was forcing it onto me. I could feel her power surrounding me as I saw through her eyes, a shadow in her existence as she held hands with another god and the world blossomed in between them.

The world grew larger and larger, and they floated above it, their power surrounding me as they created the world from fire and lava and earth. Water came next, pooling into oceans. I could sense the years it took them for the casting, and the complete faith and love that she had for this god.

His name is Hope, she whispered to me, knowing I was there as she dragged me through her past. As the world became recognizable, the two fell toward it, pulling me along through the fire and heat of the atmosphere. It burned, but their magic protected us. As we floated towards the world, Fate's stomach seemed to grow larger, as though she was pregnant.

When we landed gently on a cloud, Fate pushed me.

I fell backwards, arms flailing as her power released me. I thought I was going to hit my head on the hard floor, but Chester caught me, his magic burning against my back. I scrambled away from him as soon as I could get my feet underneath me, backing away from them both.

Trembling, I felt panic threatening to overwhelm me. It was hard to focus and yet, everything was so vivid. I was breathing hard and my clothes were slightly damp. I drew on the power in my ring, burning myself in an effort to force the world back into the orderly reality that I'd always known.

"Thank goodness," Fate said, sensing my thoughts and heading back to her desk. "It normally takes the others ages to believe. I think even now some of them still doubt." She sounded wistful, and Chester gave her a dark look.

I didn't want to get close to her again. I wanted to

run as far and as fast as I could, but I didn't know where I was, I didn't know how to get a cairn, and I wasn't any closer to my goal.

That thought focused me. I had a mission to accomplish. I didn't know what my entire plan was yet, but I had an end goal of giving a stone to Drekvic, and I was one step closer. I could listen to what they said and find an opportunity to take what I needed. Then I'd find a way to leave.

Fate looked impatient, and I sat down in one of the cushioned chairs across the desk from her. Chester visibly relaxed as he stepped forward and put his hands on the back of the chair next to me.

"It's too dangerous for her to be here," Chester said when Fate had settled herself.

"It is dangerous, but just the right amount," she replied, laughing.

"I don't think you're taking this seriously, Fate" he growled, sending chills down my spine.

She stopped laughing immediately and put both of her long-fingered hands on the desk. Her eyes flashed a darker violet, and her mouth was a straight line. Chester didn't flinch, but I saw the slight trembling in his fingers out of the corner of my eye.

"I take it extremely seriously. I led her to Melo so that she would come to me," Fate said.

Even more questions popped up in my head, but I was afraid to ask. If she had led me to Melo, did that mean she had led Drekvic to my sister? Did she know that I was trying to steal a stone?

"Then you can send her home," Chester replied, crossing his arms and glowering.

"No. Once they enter the spirit world there is no hope for them to leave," Fate replied. "There are no accounts of someone leaving this land intact unless

49

they are passing through to the Beyond."

My pulse quickened as her words sank in. My mother had just lost Jana and then I vanished into thin air. The pain in my chest made me double over in my chair as I grabbed my arms to try to hug all of the emotions inside of me. I didn't care that I probably looked weak. I felt like an soda can being crumpled under someone's boot, and I wanted nothing more than to have a do over of the past hour.

"You can do it, Fate. You have enough power," Chester insisted, his voice worried. I felt his hand rest gently on my shoulder, warmth seeping from his touch.

"I said, no," Fate snapped. "For now, she has to stay."

"I have other responsibilities. I can't watch her." His voice had a desperate ring to it, making me wish I could curl into an even tighter ball.

I heard Fate's chair squeak as she stood up, and I looked, trying to take deep breaths to combat the pressure. Her hair was floating in the currents of her magic. All of the opal stones on her dress and in her golden curls turned a blinding white.

"You will stay by her side," she commanded. When she spoke I heard other voices, layering over hers. "You will guard this girl with your life, and if anything should harm her in any way, I will hold you personally responsible." A bell rang in the distance, a single bong of noise and then a long resonance that faded into silence.

A chill ran down my back as the echo vanished. Fate had just evoked a powerful spell, and I didn't like how my mouth had gone suddenly dry as the power slowly receded from her fingertips.

Chester took a step back, his face looking pale.

"Her life before my own," he whispered. "I got it. Come on, Ellie."

Fate was still angry and I still had more questions, but after what she'd just done to Chester, I didn't want to be anywhere near her. I stood up, trying not to let my knees tremble as I scurried to the elevator in front of my new bodyguard.

I looked back at her before the doors closed completely. She was doubled over, laughing.

CHAPTER SIX

The extra bedroom was too stark for my tastes. The wooden floor had no rugs and the bed was an antique, with a metal frame that had been painted white at some point, but was now peeling. The walls were a boring gray and the only spot of color was an old wooden dresser in the corner. Each drawer was painted a different color, contrasting brightly with the pale room.

At least it had a window, and I pulled my plain wooden chair away from the corner to sit in front of it. I stared out the window into the glittering city and silently cried.

I had abandoned my mother. She would never know what happened to me and I had no way of telling her. My crusade to save Jana's soul seemed hopeless. I still had no idea how to get a stone. I was mad at my sister. Jana had made the deal knowing full well what would happen if she didn't succeed. She knew better, and here I was trying to save her from the hole that she had put herself in to.

I felt magic behind me as someone entered the room. I rubbed my face, trying to wipe away the remaining tears before I turned to face Chester. He had hovered all day yesterday as he showed me his house and tried to find something for me to do in the spartan space.

I was about to tell him to leave me alone when I turned to find it wasn't Chester at all.

Drekvic stood in the middle of the room, emitting energy that floated seductively across my skin. He looked good in this world, his black hair curling slightly around his face. His pale blue eyes seemed softer than before, but no less piercing. The power around him was tangible. I could see his black aura clinging to the edges of his ebony suit. It was disconcerting, and I didn't know what to make of it.

I slid carefully out of the chair, wanting to be on my feet and ready for anything. I didn't trust the siekewa, and I was scared that he was here to do something that would make matters worse.

"I am impressed," he said, his rich voice soft, as though he didn't want anyone to overhear us.

"Why?" I queried, reaching up and brushing away a stray hair that wasn't actually there. My fingers trembled, so I clenched them into fists to hide it.

"You are in the spirit world, my dear," he laughed, moving close enough for me smell him. The damp ash and sulfur smell tickled my nose and made me want to sneeze. "You are so close to my stone! I just wanted to let you know that I am pleased."

"Well, you can just go back to wherever you came from," I snapped. "I'm going home the first chance I get. This place is crazy and my mom probably thinks I'm dead." I crossed my arms, refusing to take a step back from him.

He touched my face and I shuddered at the influx of power. His magic wasn't as strong as Fate's, and I was able to stand under his touch. His history was shrouded, and I only got bits and pieces. I was glad.

"I could... help you with that," he crooned, his voice becoming seductive. "I could let her know where you are, that you will be home soon."

"I'm sure you would," I snarled, "for the price of my soul, right?"

He laughed and dropped his fingers.

"You are so distrustful, little witch." He walked over to the dresser and opened a drawer making a noise of disgust and closing it again. All the drawers were empty; I had checked.

"What do you want?" I demanded, trying not to think about the fact that Chester could walk in at any moment.

"I was just thinking," he said, turning around to look in the small closet that was also empty. "I want the stone, but once you get it for me, there is no reason for our relationship to end."

"Once you release Jana, I will have nothing left to say to you." I turned the chair to face the room and sat down, crossing my legs and watching him.

He was completely relaxed as he explored the room, taking in the meager furnishings with intense interest. I wondered if he had ever been in a collector's home before.

"That is where we disagree," he said, finding something of interest in the back of the closet and stepping behind the sliding door. I didn't like not being able to see what he was doing. I carefully laid my hands on my raised knee. I would not fidget.

"You see," he said, coming out of the closet with a horrendously ugly scarf wrapped around his neck. The bright orange color did nothing for his complexion, but he seemed pleased with the thing. "I have taken a liking to you. You are resourceful, competent, and I think you are exceedingly attractive."

"What?" I asked, unconsciously putting both feet back on the floor and dropping my hands to the armrests. I had already started to push myself up before I realized I'd moved and forced myself to sit back down.

"You heard me. Don't fish for compliments," he said, adjusting the scarf so it was hanging evenly on both sides of his shoulders. "I want to start a relationship with you, one that is more meaningful than you getting me a stone to free your sister."

"I just told you that once Jana is free, we are done. Why would you think I'd change my mind?" I demanded, my muscles tensing.

"It's not another deal," Drekvic said, a scowling. "I want you, Ellie. I want a relationship with you that is built on mutual trust and understanding. Your qualifications exactly meet my needs and I have every intention of pursuing you. I wanted to make that clear before I tried anything."

I stood up too fast, making my vision blur. A siekewa for a boyfriend? I couldn't believe he was even suggesting it. I would never date anyone that stole a person's soul for favors, and that he thought I would was slightly insulting.

"Absolutely not," I replied, shaking my head and stepping behind the chair so that there was more between us.

"Don't be such a tease," he admonished, snapping his fingers and creating a black top-hat with an orange ribbon that matched the ugly scarf. He looked ridiculous wearing the hat, the hideous scarf, and a smart black suit.

"What on earth are you doing?" I asked, gesturing to the scarf and hat.

"You don't think it suits me? I am fond of this color," he said, looking perplexed at my question.

"No, it's… really ugly," I said, noticing a dark stain on one end of the scarf.

He made a grumbling noise and, with another snap of his fingers, the scarf and the hat were gone—along with the rest of his suit. He was naked except for the dark silk briefs that left nothing to the imagination.

Heat rose from the tips of my toes all the way to the top of my head. I turned away, forgetting for a moment what he was and trying not to think about how perfectly sculpted his chest was or how broad his shoulders were.

"What, this is worse?" he demanded, sounding extremely amused, and also too close.

I whirled around, keeping my head up and refusing to look below his collarbone.

"Get out," I hissed, pulling on the magic in my reservoir that had recharged over night. I had slept well, and it was dying to get out into the world.

"Not until you promise me something," he said, his blue eyes soft and earnest.

I shook my head, stepping away from him and bumping into the wall; it was closer than I thought it was. He was so near that I could taste the texture of his magic and I was shaking. He couldn't take my soul, but that didn't mean he couldn't do something else.

"Get out," I repeated, but my voice failed me. It was hardly a whisper.

"Don't fall in love with that guide out there," he said, his voice a seductive purr as he reached out and put a hand on the side of my neck.

His power flowed into me, familiar at this point.

"Fate brought him to you for a reason." As he

spoke, he put his free hand on the other side of my neck, twining his fingers in my hair.

"Let go of me," I warned, ashamed that my voice trembled. My body was responding to his power in ways that I didn't understand, and I pulled more magic out of the sapphire ring, trying to push away the sensation.

"Promise me, Ellie."

"No!" I hissed, trying to slip underneath his arm. I wanted to put some space between us, at least the bed, but his grip became firm and he leaned against me, crushing me into the wall.

I moaned as he pulled every last drop of power from me. It hurt, and I wanted to start crying as my vision became blurry around the edges. His body was flush against mine, making it difficult to breathe.

"I cannot steal your soul, Ellie," he whispered. "That's part of our deal." His breath was tickling my ear and I could feel his lips brushing my skin as he talked. His power was suffocating me. Without my magic to buffer it, I could feel the clammy texture of him, overpowering my sense of self.

I gasped for air, trying not to cry. My hands were on his arms, and his skin was so cold my fingers were starting to go numb.

"If you won't make me that promise, I will take that choice from you. From now on, Ellie, the only person that will be able to survive you will be me. You will kill or injure anyone else that you fall in love with for the rest of your life."

He stroked my hair as he talked, and I shuddered at the weight of his curse, trying to dig itself into my soul.

"No," I whimpered, feeling it wrap around my right arm and cling to my skin.

"You will come to me, Ellie. I promise."

"No!" I cried, remembering the sapphire ring on my hand. The power exploded into me as I drew on the gemstone, shoving Drekvic back with all I had. He let go of me and laughed as I desperately tried to burn away his curse. It wasn't coming off, curling from my elbow to my wrist. I tried to get underneath it, but it was flush against my skin.

There was a noise in the hall and the door slammed open. Drekvic vanished with a pop of sound. I stood there dumbly as Chester came into the room, his energy sword glowing with vengeance and an extremely worried expression on his face.

When he saw me, my hair floating in the waves of my magic, he paused and lowered his weapon.

I allowed myself to slide down the wall, sobs rising up my throat of their own accord as my knees crumpled until I was sitting in an ungraceful heap on the floor, rubbing my right arm. I couldn't get the curse off.

Chester moved forward, checking, the closet and the small bathroom before letting his sword vanish. He came towards me quickly and I found I couldn't look away from his serious face. My breathing was erratic, and I couldn't tell if the panic overwhelming me was because of what Drekvic had done or because I couldn't get enough air in my lungs.

He knelt down and reached out to touch my shoulder, his hand warm against my frozen skin, and it made me shiver even harder. I released the flow of magic and tried to focus on my breathing.

"Ellie, what happened? Did he touch you? Why was there a siekewa in my house?" he said, his voice gentle but firm.

I wanted to answer, but only managed a choked

sob when I forced myself to speak. I lowered my head and closed my eyes, letting the reality of my situation crush me. Drekvic had cursed me to destroy anything that I loved. He had promised that I would go to him. Would it be out of desperation or desire? It scared me that I couldn't say for sure.

"Shh, Ellie, I won't let him hurt you," Chester said softly, moving to sit next to me. He put an arm around my shoulders, pulling me off balance and into his chest. I adjusted so I wouldn't fall, but I didn't pull away.

"He cursed me," I managed to choke, trying to bite back the tears. I held up my arm, the thing heavy as it tried to meld into my skin. I couldn't see it, but I could feel it, and the energy radiating off of it made me queasy.

"What did he say?" Chester asked in a worried voice. He reached out and took my arm, studying it intently.

"He said that if I ever fell in love with anyone I would kill them. He said that I would go to him one day. He…" I didn't want to admit it out loud, but if I didn't finish, Chester would just ask to hear the rest. "He said that he wanted to be with me… in a relationship." I shuddered, unable to help myself.

"Hey," Chester said, his voice soft but insistent, "I can help you."

I looked up at him, but he wasn't looking at my face. He was tracing the middle finger of his right hand along the length of the curse, green magic glowing.

He talked as he worked, his emerald magic seeming to shrivel Drekvic's curse.

"A curse like that will only work if you believe in it. It's magic based on conviction, and if your will is stronger than his; it can't become part of you."

"How can you be sure?" I whispered, hope rising wildly in my chest.

"Because he didn't have time to do a full ritual, and this one, while tenacious, is not buried into your soul. It's just on the surface. See?" He pinched his thumb and forefinger together over the rope-like magic and it fell away as he pulled it completely off my arm.

I watched in fascination as he pulled a pen out of thin air, his magic making it solid. He drew a circle on the floor and dropped the curse inside of it, made some hand motions, and the inside of the circle exploded.

I flinched, looking away and squinting as bright spots danced in my vision.

"It's gone," Chester said, brushing his hands together like he was shaking dirt off them. "You're not going to hurt anyone by loving them. I promise."

I gave him a faint smile and felt the tension ease from my shoulders.

"Why didn't you come when he drained all my power?" I asked, not really upset, but wanting to think of something else.

"You've been playing with your magic all day. I didn't realize it was any different until you drew on your reservoir and I sensed something else. Who is he?"

"He—he took my sister's soul. I'm trying to free her, and now I think his taking my sister was all a ruse. He made her payment impossible so I would have to get involved. I just don't know what to do now." I wanted to tell him I was scared, but I was already embarrassed by my own emotional theatrics, so I bit my lip and said nothing.

"If your sister made a bargain with the siekewa,

then even a guide can't save her. There's nothing to be done for her," Chester said, his voice sad.

"I can't give up," I whispered, a heaviness settling in my chest. I didn't want to tell him I'd already made a deal with Drekvic.

"And it seems Fate doesn't want you to, since she won't send you home," Chester said, leaning back against the wall and sighing.

"I wanted to ask her more questions, but she is intimidating." I shuddered, thinking of the way her voice changed when she cursed Chester to be my protector. I heard the bell ringing in my ears and shook my head to clear away the memory before it frightened me again.

"Yeah, she was pretty angry, huh?" he asked, chuckling to himself.

He massaged the back of his neck, looking thoughtful.

"Are you okay?" he asked, studying me out of the corner of his eye.

"I'll be fine," I responded. I stood up, not wanting to be so close to him anymore. "I just worry about my mom. She just lost Jana, and now she's probably going to think I'm dead too."

"Your mom will be fine," he said, standing up and brushing off the back of his dark jeans. "I checked her soul's collection date. It's not for a long time."

"Why would you do that?" I demanded, turning back to look at him. I was horrified he knew when she was supposed to die, but also relieved that it wouldn't be for a while.

"I was supposed to be your collector. You're so well-adjusted, I couldn't figure out what would happen to you. I wanted to make sure it wasn't because your mother and sister died together. Since there was no collection for your sister, I knew that it wasn't planned." He shrugged. "I like to research."

"Was mine planned?"

"Yes. I've known about you for a long time."

It made me uneasy, like there was something I was supposed to know but couldn't quite figure it out. I thought about Chester and how he researched my family's demise. It would make sense that there was a schedule to keep things running smoothly. It was a schedule that Chester could no longer fulfill because he was watching me.

The silence stretched, feeling awkward. I turned away to look out the window.

"Are you hungry? I can show you around the city. We can get something to eat."

I nodded absently, realizing that I hadn't eaten since before I saw Melo the day before.

"I just--need some time to freshen up," I said, running a hand up to touch my messy braid. I had really freaked out, and I couldn't look directly at him.

"It sounds silly if you've never done it before, but if you talk to the closet while the door is closed, it'll make clothes appear when you open it. You just have to ask for what you want. The--dresser can make items appear, like soap or fresh linens for your bed. I'm not sure how long you'll be staying here, but I'd like you to be comfortable. If you need anything, just let me know."

"Thanks," I said, wishing he'd told me the night before. I wouldn't have slept in my underwear.

He gave me a tentative smile and then nodded. He left the room silently, shutting the door behind him. It was with a tired shuffle that I moved towards the small bathroom, but not before I asked the dresser for some shampoo.

CHAPTER SEVEN

Chester took me to see the city. I allowed myself to be drawn into the sights, knowing that once I got Drekvic his stone, I'd never see this place again, and it really was beautiful. The buildings weren't actually made of glass, as it wasn't brittle or delicate. It was smooth under my fingers as I ran my hand along the door frame of the store, but I couldn't actually see through it.

The inside of the shop was modern, with lots of open space and sparse shelves. The clothing was piled in perfect squares, and the ones that were hanging on the racks had space between each one. No one was inside the store, and I looked around, confused. There was a dressing room in the back, but no one manning the place. I didn't see a cashier or employee in sight. Noticing my confused look, Chester gave me the smallest of smiles.

"It's all for flavor here," he explained. "Anything we want, we can just get with magic, so there's really no need to barter for clothes."

"What about food?" I asked, frowning. We'd gotten pastries and coffee earlier. Chester had ordered for us and there had been spirits serving us. They'd been interested in me, but they had a job and other things to do, so they hadn't paid us much mind. This store was completely different, and I was left feeling unsettled.

"We can make food with magic too, but it doesn't taste as good," Chester replied, shrugging. "Specialty items are often sold as well, things that you might not have the imagination or skill to create, but someone else does."

"What kind of specialty items?" I asked, touching a folded sweater. It was soft and already felt warm. I pulled my fingers away, walking towards the shoes on the back shelves.

"Special jewelry," Chester explained, following me. "Artwork, games, toys."

I couldn't imagine Chester buying anything as frivolous as a toy, but there had been collectors that looked really young. I wondered if they grew older or if once they became a collector they just stopped. Would it be rude to ask? Age was always a touchy subject, but if they didn't age, was it quite so dangerous? I didn't know, so erred on the side of saying nothing.

"What's your favorite thing to buy?" I asked, kneeling down to get a better look at a pair of heels that looked like they were made of glass. I wondered if they had fairy tales that had to do with pumpkins and princesses in glass slippers here too. Their entire city seemed to be made of crystals, so maybe this place was where the story originated from.

"Are you getting tired?" Chester asked, his voice full of concern as he completely ignored my question.

He'd been a jerk when I first came to the spirit world, but since the incident with Drekvic, Chester had been nothing but kind to me. The siekewa seemed to bring out the protector side of the collector, and now I was under that umbrella. I wanted to say I didn't need his protection, but I was just being vain. I needed all the help I could get, and we both knew it.

"A little bit," I replied, scratching my chin absently as I stood up. I hadn't slept well, and the stress was taking its toll on my body.

"There's one other place I'd like to take you, before we head back," Chester said, turning back to the door. I followed him, glancing back one more time at the interior of the store.

"It's sad," I said, looking at the emptiness of the space. Chester paused, tilting his head in question. "Everywhere is empty, like time forgot them."

Chester said nothing, just held the door open for me. Feeling slightly melancholy, I walked past him and into the spirit world's sunshine, closing my eyes and taking a deep breath at the warmth on my face.

The last building was different from the others. It stood out starkly against the rest of the glittering city. Instead of the whimsical crystal designs that I had gotten used to, this structure was made of a dark stone and designed in a simple post and lintel style. There were no arches or frills, and only a single door made of plain oak.

There were protection spells on the wood, but they felt old and lifeless. I reached out to touch one when we passed and I couldn't sense any magic left inside. The protections had been allowed to run out.

Inside was dark, with only a couple lamps lighting the space. It was large, but the light didn't seem to reach the entire length of the room and the corners were dim. There were benches lining the edges of the walls, but they looked uncomfortable. No other collector was around. The heavy silence made me move slightly closer to Chester.

"This is one of the most important rooms in the city," he said, his voice echoing in the hard space. "It's where we anoint new collectors and give them a cairn." He reached up to touch the stone on his throat.

"Then why isn't it protected?" I asked, gesturing to the defunct magic on the door.

"It doesn't need to be," he replied. "This way."

He moved toward the only other door in the room, directly across from us. We had to walk over a low wooden riser, where I was guessing they had the ceremony.

The other room was long, but very narrow. The walls were ten feet apart and lined with shelves that stretched the entire length of the room, far enough away that I could barely see them. Each shelf had neat glass boxes lined with velvet. In each box there was a stone.

"This is where we store the cairns," he said, his voice low and respectful.

I moved forward, realizing now where I would be able to get my stone. There was no protection here. I could just walk in and take one the moment I was able to sneak away from Chester. It would be simple to call Drekvic and then Jana would be free.

I wouldn't think any further past that, as I was dreading my next encounter with him. I also didn't want to think about what he'd be able to do once he had a cairn. Was I making a terrible mistake? I didn't want to think about that, either, so I walked past Chester into the room, admiring the cairns and wondering what exactly they were.

The power humming off of them was admirable, and I felt different frequencies and textures as I passed each one. Chester didn't stop me as I reached out to pick up a glass case. It wasn't too heavy, and the lid was easy enough to lift.

"Don't touch the stone itself," he said, and I almost dropped the box when I realized that he was hovering right behind me.

"Stop sneaking up on me!" I hissed, getting a firmer grip on the slippery glass.

"I can't help that your ears are so closed to me," he replied, laughing. He reached into the case to pull out the cairn so I could see it better.

"How come you can touch it?" I asked, turning my head to look at the swirling patterns.

"If you touch the stone, you enter into an agreement with it," he explained. "My cairn protects me, so I don't have any issues. You are unattached, so if you wake it up and all you tell it is that you wanted to get a better look, it'll get mad and reject you. That can be very painful."

"It's sentient?" I asked, looking at the pink and green swirls this one was emitting.

"To an extent. They're made for the collectors. They help us pass through the gates. As you've seen, the magic from the cairns can be made solid to create things, like my sword, or in the case of the gates, their keys. They recharge slowly, but have so much energy that it's difficult to ever use it up. When that happens though, we just have to come here, put it to rest and pick up a new one."

He put the stone back onto the velvet, arranging it so the black cord was in a simple circle like before. He took the box and put it back on the shelf.

"I've always thought they were very pretty. I thought you would like to see them."

"They're beautiful," I replied.

My palms were starting to sweat. I had never

broken the law before. I'd never stolen anything--not even free samples. I didn't want to steal anything from the collectors either, but family was family. I wouldn't let Jana be used. I would pay the price.

"Why aren't these protected?" I asked, pushing my plans to the back of my head. I would worry about it later.

"Like I said, they don't need to be. Only those that are worthy of taking a stone can enter this room," he said, smiling at me. Apparently I was worthy, but I wasn't trying to be a collector, just save my sister.

I looked at the long room again, wondering whether or not I'd be able to steal a stone and make it out to a place where I could summon Drekvic without being caught. A fierce longing rose in my chest. I wanted to go home and curl up on my familiar couch with a cup of hot chocolate and Jana reading a book beside me.

Recognizing that I was ready to leave, Chester gestured to the door and we headed out of the cairn room. I was tired and not paying much of attention, so when he stopped suddenly in my path, I walked into him.

I almost swore at him, but I could feel how tense tense his shoulders were. I peeked around his arm to find a woman.

She was a siekewa with the same dark hair and pale skin as Drekvic. Her eyes were the same ice blue, unnerving against her dark lashes. She didn't look as gaunt or as frail as Drekvic, but I could smell the faint hint of ash on her skin. She wore a black coat, unbuttoned, over a white mini-dress. Her white boots went up to her thigh and had a small heel that clicked as she came to a stop in front of Chester. She was tall, and I didn't like that I had to look up at her.

I wondered why Chester wasn't drawing his sword when I noticed the small white stone nestled against the hollow of her throat. She was a collector?

"Rakshina," Chester said, nodding his head in greeting. His voice was surly, and I could tell he didn't like her.

Why would a siekewa be in a special building wearing a collector's stone? Was that why Drekvic wanted a stone? Did he want to be a collector, too?

"Mr. Sandsil," she responded, nodding her head graciously. Her voice was high and airy, almost like a child's. "I thought I felt one of my kin with the stones. It worried me, so I came to check."

"Just us," he replied, stepping aside toward gesture to me. "This is Ellie Alwood. She is my guest."

Rakshina seemed to glide forward, extending her hand to me. Chester moved to stop me from touching her. Unruffled, Rakshina just shrugged.

"You still do not trust me?"

"I doubt I ever will," Chester replied, and I wondered what the story was between these two.

"Fair enough. Ms. Alwood, it has been a brief pleasure. If you ever would like to speak, I live on the edge of the city." She gave me a knowing look that seemed to lay all my secrets bare. I knew with certainty that she could see Drekvic's mark on me.

With a wave, she walked out of the hall, her heels clicking on the stone. The door shut silently behind her.

I raised an eyebrow at Chester, but he just shook his head.

"It's better if you don't associate with people like her, especially if you've already got a siekewa following you."

"Are a lot of the collectors siekewa?" I asked,

worried that I might run into more of them.

"Just that one," he replied. "Let's go."

Instead of following Rakshina out the door, he reached out and took my hand. The teleportation wasn't as terrifying this time, but I still didn't like the sensation, and doubted I would ever get used to it.

We landed on a circle near Chester's home and he led the way back in silence. I wondered if he was annoyed with me or at our unexpectedly meeting Rakshina. I couldn't think of anything that I'd done, so assumed it must have been the siekewa.

We didn't talk until we reached his house and he started preparing something for dinner, thoughtfully remembering that I needed to eat more often than he did. It had been amusing to watch him struggle in the door yesterday with several large grocery bags, announcing that he didn't know what witches ate.

"Rakshina isn't a bad collector," he said, looking up at me after pulling some lettuce out of his fridge. "She has a dark history, but she has never given us cause to doubt the sincerity in her change of profession."

"Then why don't you like her?" I asked, flopping down on the uncomfortable couch.

"I don't trust her," he replied. "I don't trust her kind as a matter of habit. They're always up to something, always have a hidden motive. She's been a collector for a hundred years now, but siekewa are long-lived. They don't always think in terms of here and now. She could be biding her time, just waiting for us to let our guard down."

He chopped the lettuce as he spoke, using more force than strictly necessary. He was agitated, moving his shoulders in time with his chopping.

I tried to adjust myself on the couch, feeling a

spring dig into my hips. It hurt, and I gave up, standing and moving to the stool on the high counter.

"Why don't you get new furniture?" I grumbled, not wanting to talk about Rakshina anymore.

"I need new furniture?" he asked, looking up in surprise.

"That couch is terrible and that end table looks older than my mother," I complained.

"It probably is," he admitted. "I haven't changed much in the last two-hundred years. I don't think about it."

I wondered what it felt like to live long enough to forget that other things wear down. I twisted my ring around on my hand, thinking about past and future. There were no child collectors. I wondered if that was because they had been kept hidden from me or if there weren't any to begin with.

"Where are all the kids?" I asked, looking up at him.

There was an almost imperceptible tightening of his shoulders, and his eyes closed for a moment longer than a blink. His chopping slowed, becoming deliberate and careful. If I hadn't been watching him when I asked the question, I wouldn't have noticed the change.

"The spirit guides are made, not born," he said, his voice deep and soft. "Once we choose this path, we can no longer have children and we lose our past. We still have intimacy and love, but our bodies are… frozen, you could say. We don't age and we can't reproduce."

"Made?" I asked, my natural curiosity ignoring his warning flags.

"Remember the cairn hall?" he asked, turning away from me so he could wash some cherry tomatoes in the sink. I wondered if he'd be offended that I didn't eat them.

"They go there to be changed?"

"It's usually people like you that can see us already. There are two recruiters that approach your kind in the spirit world if they think you have the right morals. Once chosen, we offer the chance to live forever. Most turn us down, but every fifteen years or so someone that accepts and we have a cairn ceremony. Fate uses her power to change their bodies so they can survive on the spirit plane, and the stone makes a bargain with them to serve."

"So you made that choice?" I asked. I couldn't imagine leaving my family behind.

"The reasons we have for making our choices are very personal, Ellie," he admonished gently. "I know you're curious, but it's not something I like to talk about."

I blushed, looking down at his hands to see that he was now cutting up leftover chicken into strips and placing them neatly on the salad. He set it in front of me along with a side of balsamic vinaigrette. It was nice having someone take care of me, and I wondered if I should hire a chef when I got back home... if I ever made it back home.

"I forgot to buy croutons," Chester said suddenly, his brow furrowing. "Witches like croutons, right?"

"This witch doesn't," I replied, smiling at his concern.

"Well, it works out then," he replied, washing his cutting board and knife.

"There's a festival?" I asked, noting the calendar on the wall to my left. The day after tomorrow had *Solstice Festival* neatly written in its little box.

"Yes," he said, scrubbing a stubborn piece of

chicken off the bamboo board. "Normally I would be helping, but Fate has requested I suspend all my other duties." He sounded irritated, and I wondered if he was upset that he couldn't help with the festival or about having to take a break from being a soul guide.

"I'd like to go," I said, taking a bite of the crunchy salad.

"Well, then we can go," he replied, walking around to the couch and poking it gingerly. He made a face and sighed before sitting down. Could a collector be self-conscious?

The festival would be the perfect time to steal the cairn. If it was anything like the festivities at home, losing Chester in the bustling crowds would be easy. The plan made the sweet dressing sour in my mouth. I didn't like deceit, but my mind was set. Jana was my little sister, and since our father died when we were young, I had been her care-taker while Mother was out working to pay the bills. It was my job to make sure Jana got to school on time and remembered to brush her teeth. I taught her how to ride a bike and would soothe her hurts when she scraped her knees. When I learned to read, we would stay up late and hide under the covers and I would read to her and teach her. I wasn't about to let Jana's soul wither away. Regardless of what it meant, I would save her.

"Who knows," Chester said, oblivious to my thoughts, "you might be home before then."

"I thought the only way to get home was for Fate to send me back?"

"That's the only way I can think of, but maybe there is another way." He lay down on the couch and gestured at the ceiling, his long legs hanging off the side. "There are places where the way to reality is thinner than others. If you remember how you got here, maybe you can go back the same way."

"I don't think I can. I was using a stone. Melo said it would only work one way, which was why she had never tried to use it before."

"What kind of stone was it?" he asked, sitting up a little so he could look at me.

"It was a cairn, but... fake?" I said, shrugging. I plucked a cherry tomato out of the salad and bit into it. The insides squished across my tongue and I forced myself to swallow instead of gag. I'd throw the rest in the trash.

"There is no key for the first gate, which is why we can't enter your reality. Only souls can make the trip when their body dies. What your friend had must be extremely dangerous to take you the whole way through the veil."

"She drew a spiral around it," I supplied, wondering if that was important.

"You know another siekewa?" he asked, sitting up abruptly.

I looked at him, confused. "She was a shape-shifter," I replied, feeling defensive.

Siekewa weren't the only creatures that used spirals in their magic. It wasn't super common, but spirals tended to draw things out. I used them when I had a cold and wanted to draw the virus out of me. They were tricky and could be dangerous, but it wasn't inherently bad magic.

"Putting a cairn in a spiral is forbidden. You're lucky that it was fake."

"What does it do?"

He shook his head and lay back down, once again gesturing with his hands towards the ceiling. "Fate tells us that putting a cairn in a spiral will draw all its energy out and release it into the world all at once. It's dangerous and can have fatal consequences. That much energy could break the barriers between realities and combine all three realities. It would be chaos."

That was terrifying. Did Drekvic want to change reality? Could I really give him the cairn if he did? I tried to hide my nerves by continuing to eat, but I couldn't taste anything. I wondered what else Drekvic would be willing to bargain for the stone and decided I'd rather not think about it.

I remembered the feel of his body pressed against me as he tried to force me into submission and I felt sick. I put my fork down, barely able to sallow the bite in my mouth. Would he let Jana go if I agreed to be his? Was that something I could even live with? I shuddered. I would stick to the original bargain. If I broke something, I'd just have to fix it later.

After dinner, I went to my room to rest. I didn't lock the door, although I wanted to. I felt raw and uncertain, and I needed to make a plan.

I went to the dresser and asked for a journal to write in, and I sat down on the bed with my legs crossed. I hadn't specified what type of journal I wanted, so this one was spiral-bound with thick covers. It was perfect for sitting without a desk, making me wonder if the dresser was more than just magical.

I wrote down everything I knew so far. Fate had sent Chester to pick me up, but I was still unsure of what part she played in my coming to the spirit world in the first place. Chester had told me about the cairn hall and I knew I could get in, but transporting a cairn might be more difficult. If anyone could just walk in, too many people would have the chance to notice an entire glass case missing. If I just took the stone itself, it would be assumed that someone had taken it out into the field.

I couldn't touch them, though. I could use tongs, but then what would I transport it in? I drew a blank line on the page, pressing harder than necessary into the paper.

I felt better.

I stood up to pace the room. It was harder to make notes while walking, but my brain worked better when I was moving, and I needed all the edge I could get.

Chester had shown me the place where festivals usually took place in our meandering earlier. It was a large open park where crowds could gather and set up tents. It was only a couple blocks from the cairn hall, as it was easy to finish a ceremony and then walk outside to celebrate.

This was good and bad. I'd be able to get inside the hall without complication, but there was also a chance that someone might find me there. I didn't see a reason for anyone else to be in the cairn hall, but it was still something I should prepare for.

My back-up plan could be that I wanted to get away from the crowds. Rakshina had sensed me with the stones, so she might come looking again. Based on how Chester treated her, though, she might not be at the festival at all.

Think, Ellie, I berated myself. This had to work or I might not get another chance.

What are your resources?

I couldn't count on Chester to help me. His loyalties were obviously to Fate and the souls. He would never help me get a cairn for Drekvic to save a single soul, even if she was my sister.

Fate liked to cause mischief, but I doubted I could count on her. I rubbed the back of my neck, sliding into a cross-legged situation on the floor, bent over to hide my face from the light.

My hair was loose and fell around my face, blocking my vision. With one sense gone, I took a deep breath, calming my nerves and trying to still my mind. I used meditation a lot in my work. Working with a bunch of college students trying to make their mark and judge my work often caused a lot of stress. Meditation was a way to center myself.

Jana's face kept interrupting.

We had been typical siblings, arguing over lots of little things, but she really had been my only friend. No matter what happened with her soul in her future lives, in this life she was dead, and I missed her.

I allowed myself a moment to experience the weight of that sorrow, let it press down on my lungs and make my limbs impossible to lift. Tears ran salty tracks down my cheeks as my breathing became labored.

It hurt, but it was enough.

I forced myself to sit up, brushing away my tears and returning to the light of the room. I left the journal on the ground as I stood up and stretched, banishing the sadness. I didn't have the luxury of grieving at length just yet.

I walked over to the dresser to ask for tissues when I realized that what I needed to solve my problem was literally sitting right in front of me. I put my hand on the smooth wood, ready for the dresser to give me exactly what I asked for.

"I need some sort of bag that will allow me to carry a cairn without touching it," I said, my voice low and still carrying a hint of grief.

I waited a moment, before opening the drawer. The pouch was a little larger than my hand. I picked it up, feeling the smooth velvet under my fingertips. I would be able to turn it inside out, pick up the cairn and wrap it in the bag without ever having to touch it with my fingers. It was small enough to fit in a purse, so I could hide it without being obvious.

All I needed was an opportunity to get away from Chester and steal the cairn.

Chester's face intruded in my plan, looking embarrassed at how worn down his furniture was. My hand was moving back to the drawer to put the bag away before I realized it. I stopped myself, clutching the velvet pouch tightly in a fist.

I didn't have a choice. I hated to betray Chester, especially after all he'd done for me so far, but Jana was family.

I closed the drawer and walked back to the bed, scooping the journal up as I went. I'd made my choice.

CHAPTER EIGHT

Chester's shoulder was warm underneath my fingers, his dark red shirt a constant beacon of safety in the crowd. He was walking ahead of me, making a path for us as we wound our way through the throng of collectors and spirits.

The festival was more chaotic than I had imagined. Not only were the collectors out in full force, there were also spirits in attendance. I was fascinated by them.

Each spirit represented a core element. Chester stopped at a stall being run by a large, mostly human-shaped earth spirit with legs the girth of tree trunks. When we stopped, his smell of rich soil mixed with rotting leaves wafted over me. His magic signature was like nothing I'd ever seen before, and it was all I could do to resist the urge to ask him whether or not I could study him. He was selling carvings, small knick-knacks that would have been common place at any fair back home. Chester, however, was asking about end tables. I pursed my lips together to keep from giggling.

I let Chester talk while I looked around. There were a lot of collectors, but the spirits stole the show.

The water spirits varied from giant blobs rolling through the crowd like huge slugs of water to small sprites that floated on the wind, sprinkling rain wherever they went. Each spirit seemed unique, and their magic was potent.

They seemed to find me as interesting as I found them. A lot kept taking backward glances at me, or just outright stared. I couldn't always tell where their faces were, but I felt their magic checking me out.

A wind sprite that looked like a small pink fairy stopped in front of me. Her face was scrunched up, confused.

"What are you?" she demanded, reaching out with a tiny hand like she wanted to touch me.

Her magic tried to curl into my nose, making me sneeze.

Chester broke off his conversation with the carpenter to wave a dismissive hand at the fairy. The displaced air of his gesture caught her wings, pushing her back. She said something under her breath and flew away, turning back and throwing one more shot of magic at me, trying to get me to breathe it.

I blocked it, not liking her aggression.

"It's because you're not dead," the earth spirit grumbled, his voice sounding like gravel.

Chester nodded at the spirit and said that he would be in touch before pulling me away from the stall and back into the throng.

"How come everyone can tell I'm not dead?" I asked, obviously unable to tell the difference myself.

Chester smiled and pulled me to the side of a colorful tent. A large tree spirit strode by, clearly not paying attention to where it was putting its big feet. It would have crushed us if we hadn't moved.

"We're not like humans, witches, or other

supernatural creatures. People who live in the spirit world see things in terms of energy. To us, you're a glittering source of it. The blood that pumps through your veins is alive and your beating heart pulses. It's distracting. Spirits and collectors will be drawn to you like children to rainbows."

His voice was low and melodic, and I felt my pulse quicken as he talked. I swallowed the lump in my throat, completely distracted by his nearness.

"Let's go over there," he said, not noticing the redness in my cheeks. He pointed toward another booth and we headed over. As bright as I must have been, I was still jostled in the crowd. Chester's reassuring hand was on my shoulder, keeping me steady. I was grateful that he was watching my back.

The booth Chester had directed me to was some type of game. There were four baskets against the far wall, and on the counter across from it were baskets of balls. The trick was to get the balls into the basket without using your hands—it was a test of magic. Since so many people used their hands for gestures of power, the floor by the clerk was littered with failed attempts.

I smiled, thinking it would be a fun exercise, and handed the clerk a silver token. Chester chose not to play, and was watching our surroundings instead.

It was kind of exhausting to be guarded all the time, but I understood his precaution. If I was a beacon in the spirit world, it would be easy for someone to follow and overpower me.

Three other collectors signed up for the game, and I glanced over at my competition. Two of them looked like twins, teenagers with unruly brown hair and big matching grins. The other looked familiar, with blonde hair and blue eyes. He gave me an appreciative look and raised his eyebrows.

I pursed my lips in what I hope looked like a tight smile and turned away. I was wearing a modestly cut, but flattering, black dress, and my exposed legs were cold. I was glad my arms were covered from shoulder to elbow, because I was blushing. All the attention was starting to get to me.

The clerk rang his bell and I had to pull myself together to focus. I reached for the extra energy in my sapphire, knowing that it would be steadier than the flighty stuff floating high on my emotions. I kept my hands resting lightly on the table where they could be seen, and delicately pushed the red ball at the top of my pile to make it float. It popped into the air easily enough and I continued to push gently to move it across the open space. Halfway across the distance, my grip on the power faltered, and I had to stop myself from using my hands to strengthen the connection.

Telekinesis was one of Jana's specialties. I was better at biological magic, more sympathetic in nature. It tended to act on living things, using their own energy to help the power of the spell.

The game was difficult, and I glanced over at my competitors. The twins had dropped their balls on the ground and were laughing, but the older collector had managed to get his to the basket. It was a lonely green sphere inside the weave.

"Second ball!" the clerk called. I decided I was going to make it this time.

My next ball was yellow, and I reached out to it. Once again, getting it into the air was easy. I thought about what Jana had always told me: it was a simple matter of asking the thing to move, rather than forcing it to obey.

"People," she had lectured, "are more likely to cooperate if you ask nicely. Objects are the same. You're too forceful, Ellie."

Thoughts of Jana made me melancholy, but I politely asked the ball to land in the basket.

The ball jerked from the air, flying with great speed to land in the basket with enough force to knock the whole thing over. Chester laughed as the clerk's jaw dropped and closed again just as quickly. The other three contestants had dropped their balls when they heard the crash.

My face was on fire, and I looked down at my trembling hands.

The blonde collector leaned over to whisper in my ear.

"The spirit world itself jumps to do your bidding when you ask nicely." His breath tickled my ear, and I pulled away. There was something about his dark blue eyes that made me nervous, and I took another step to put distance between us.

The clerk was trying to set the basket up again, but the ball had torn through it in its haste to do my bidding. I furrowed my brow, hoping he didn't have to close up because of me. Chester moved forward behind the counter to help.

"I didn't think it would do that," I said to the blonde, still waiting for a response at my side.

"I figured, based on your first attempt." He gestured to the red ball, lying pathetically on the mat.

"You're good at this, though," I said, trying to direct the conversation away from me.

He shrugged, looking away from me. His smile returned when he looked back. "I'm sorry, I never introduced myself. I'm Thomas."

He held out his hand, and I didn't want to touch

him, but politeness was too ingrained. His handshake was firm and casual. He didn't try to hold onto my fingers, for which I was grateful.

Like with Chester, I saw none of his history. It seemed the collectors really did lose their past in order to have a future that went on forever.

"Ellie," I said, crossing my arms and looking at Chester and the clerk.

Chester was doing some sort of magic, weaving with his fingers as the basket put itself back together. I sighed, feeling even more embarrassed. I really had broken it.

"So, Fate brought you to us? Are you going to be a collector?" Thomas asked, eager to continue our conversation.

I wasn't sure if I wanted people to believe Fate brought me here, but I wanted to explain that I was here because my sister was an idiot even less. I just shrugged and settled in to wait for Chester to finish. If Thomas hadn't started talking to me, it would have been a good time to sneak away and steal the cairn. At this point, I wasn't sure I'd be able to do it, despite the large crowd.

"Did Chester tell you not to talk to me?" Thomas asked, sounding annoyed.

"Of course not," I replied, unable to mask the sharpness of my voice. I sighed, knowing that I couldn't leave it at that. "I'm not good at small talk."

He chuckled at that, his annoyance disappearing.

"Why would Chester tell me not to talk to you?" I demanded, trying to keep my voice low.

Thomas shrugged, but I didn't believe it. His words and face were friendly, but his body language didn't match his attitude. His actions and gestures seemed practiced. It made me wonder what it was he wanted from me.

"Chester doesn't like any of the other collectors. He's nice enough to the spirits and the souls he guides are taken care of, but the rest of us? I guess he's like you: no good at socializing."

I looked over at Chester finishing up the basket and wondered if that was true. He'd been nice enough to me, but I hadn't seen him talk to another collector as a friend. Was that why Fate had dumped him with me?

"You don't have to be like him though," Thomas was saying, although I was only half listening now. "You could always hang out with me or one of the other collectors." He kept talking, but I tuned him out, watching Chester has he said good bye to the clerk and walked back to us.

"Thomas," Chester said in greeting, stopping next to me. He was close, and I leaned into him to feel his arm brush mine. The heat was reassuring, and I felt better knowing he was close.

"Hey, Chester," Thomas replied off-handedly. "You sure have kept Ellie cloistered. Why don't we all go to the drinking booths and have some fun?"

Chester looked at me, waiting for me to respond. I didn't want to go drinking, and I certainly didn't want to hang out with Thomas. I didn't think I wanted to meet more collectors, either.

"We're okay. Thanks for the offer," I said. "I want to look around more."

"We'll be there if you change your mind," Thomas replied sourly, trying to keep the smile on his face.

I smiled as Chester put a gentle hand on my back, pulling me away from the game. I had three balls left to play, but figured the clerk wouldn't let me even if I wanted to. My mind turned over the broken basket and

how eager the ball had been to do my bidding.
Apparently there was something to Jana's advice.

We walked past a couple more stalls and noticed
the music getting louder. It was a lively tune that
reminded me a bit of folk music. It was meant for
tapping feet and dancing. Even as distracted as I was,
it was uplifting. Chester leaned over my shoulder and
pointed toward the musician.

He had several instruments, a fiddle, a drum, and
some sort of flute. He also had at least eight arms and
two heads. One head was balancing the fiddle while
two arms played it. Two arms held the flute up to the
lips of the second head, and two other hands would
occasionally beat the drum. A final pair of hands
would clap with the beat or turn pages in his music
book. The creature's nose-less faces were smiling and
everyone around him seemed to be enjoying
themselves.

"Why didn't you want to go with Thomas?" I
asked Chester now that he was close enough that I
didn't have to shout.

He didn't answer, but a decidedly mischievous
look grew in his eyes. He grabbed my hand and pulled
me to the side of the dance-floor. After pushing
through several rows of people we entered a small
garden with a fountain. We could still hear the music,
but no one was here aside from us. It was darker here.

"Watch," he breathed, excited and grinning. He
reached up to touch his cairn and it started to glow
brightly. When he pulled his fingers away they were
glowing as well, like he had dipped them in paint. He
walked around the small garden touching leaves and
flowers before running in a circle around the rim of the
fountain. Everywhere he touched had a smear of
glowing light. When he was done making stars in the

trees, he clapped his hands and the remaining magic on his fingers dispersed, floating around us like snow.

"So full of surprises!" I laughed, moving forward to be surrounded by lights. I reached out to catch one, feeling the warmth of his magic in my cupped hands. "It's pretty, even if it's an obvious distraction." I turned to him, still smiling.

His face was serious, aside from the small smile at the corner of his lips. My mirth vanished, my heart fluttering. Chester was a spirit guide. No matter how attractive I found him, and no matter how much I enjoyed spending time with him, I was going to leave the moment I could. I didn't want any loose ties. He stopped closer and held out his hand. My body reacted even though my brain was telling me not to. My hand rested gently in his as he pulled me closer.

We moved to the music. I didn't know the song or the dance, but Chester led me easily. He kept me grounded when he spun me and the warmth of his skin kept the chill of the night away. He touched me lightly, never over-stepping his bounds, but always there to grab my outstretched hand or point out his feet to show me how to step. By the time the song ended I was breathless, and laughing too hard to catch it.

A playful jig started, all footwork, and Chester tried to teach me the steps. I didn't know whether or not I wanted this moment to end.

When it did, my legs protested, so I waved him off and sat down on the edge of the fountain, taking deep breaths and wiping the sweat off my forehead. I felt dirty, but good. Jana had always made fun of me when I had told her I didn't like to sweat. She would drag me off anyway to do something active, like tennis, running, or volleyball with her college friends.

"Did my distraction work?" he asked lightly,

sitting next to me, his arm brushing mine. He was barely winded, and I scowled at the faint gleam of sweat on his forehead, barely there.

"It did until you said that," I replied, bumping into him and leaning away.

"I wanted to tell you. I just wanted time for a good answer to come to me."

"And did it?"

He nodded, smiling. I liked his smile. It was gentle and kind, nothing like Drekvic's seductive smirk.

"I'm a good soul guide. The people we take from their bodies to the afterlife are precious. Many of them have done bad things, and some of them don't believe they're good, but their soul leaves all of that behind. It's the body and the world that can turn even the best of souls into something hard and bitter." He pointed up, and for the first time I noticed the darkness of the sky.

In the inky blackness there were streaks of stars. At first glance they looked pure white, but if I was careful, I could see the edges glistening with different colors. They seemed to move in a pattern, a slow dance that flowed like a river, and it was absolutely the most beautiful thing I had ever seen. I couldn't say why, but I wanted to be there. More than anything in the world, I wanted to go up into the stars. Chester's warm hand on my arm pulled me back, and I realized that I had stood up and was on my tiptoes, hands outstretched.

Unsure of what possessed me to try to reach the stars, I turned away from him, embarrassed, but he didn't laugh.

"That is the Beyond," he whispered, his voice full of awe. "The place your soul yearns to reach, just as mine does. We can only see bits and pieces of it here, the slow dance of magic that holds our realms together."

"It's beautiful," I whispered, sitting back down and looking at my knees. I didn't want to look up again and be lost.

"When I became a collector, I gave up on ever being able to get there. I thought that duty and love were more important than moving on." He sounded sad, and when I looked back at him, I saw him swallow. He was looking at the crystallized cobblestones, his hands folded in on each other.

"Living with the collectors, I've found that I don't like my kind very much. I didn't want to go with Thomas and his friends because a lot of what they do and feel isn't real. They gave up on having a family and having children, and so gave up on making lasting connections."

He rubbed the back of his neck, looking like he was lost and remembering something that was far away from what he was actually saying.

"Not everyone is like that, of course," he went on. "I think enough of them are, though, and it's not a way to live." He looked up at me, and I was surprised to see moisture in his eyes. "I mean, I understand them. If my family and friends were dead and gone to the Beyond..."

He stood up, walking away from me to the edge of the clearing. He crossed his arms, breathing deeply and trying to control his emotions. "I'm sorry, I'm babbling."

I followed him, reaching out to loop my arm through his. He looked over at me, surprised.

"There's no need to apologize. My father died when Jana and I were young. He overdosed on magic. The only friend I had was Jana. I wanted to find a cure for addiction, and I've spent my entire life trying to find a way to make people well. The only other thing I did was take care of Jana. She needed me, and I failed her." I was embarrassed by how much I had told him, but I didn't move away from him, just looked into the glowing bushes and leaned my head on his shoulder.

"I just… I wanted to let you know that you're not as alone as you think."

"Thanks," he said, releasing my arm to hug my shoulders, pulling me into him. "You're not as weird, or alone as you think, either."

I smiled, even though he couldn't see it, and we watched his glowing lights fade from the leaves. As we stood there, side by side, I was careful not to look at the sky.

CHAPTER NINE

The air was cold on my skin and I felt naked without my sapphire ring. I had pushed all my energy into the stone and hidden it in the small garden where I had danced with Chester. With no energy and no extra storage, I felt vulnerable and tired, but it was the only thing I could think of doing to dim my shine in the spirit world.

Chester had gone to get us drinks, and I had taken the opportunity to sneak away from the garden to visit the cairn hall. Every shadow on the way as I moved through the empty street made me jump, but I had to save Jana, and not even the thought of Chester's kindness could stop me. The building loomed ahead of me, dimly lit and menacing. I slipped through the old door, almost tripping on nothing. My heart was pounding in my ears as I paused to look around the big space. What if I couldn't enter this time? Would the stones know what I was doing?

I had to try.

The walk across the dark hall seemed to take forever. I could see the faint glow from the cairn room, making it easier to pick my way around the raised platform. The door was ajar, and I walked through it without touching it.

The cairns, resting in their glass cases, were the source of the light, and I felt exposed as I pulled the velvet bag from my purse. Using the fabric as a barrier between my skin and the stone, I opened a glass case and picked the cairn up. From there it was a simple matter of twisting the bag inside out and tying off the top. I dropped it back into my purse and turned to leave.

There was a faint noise from the hall, and I felt the blood drain from my face. There were steps echoing in the outer area, and I turned and scrambled farther into the cairn room. I reached the end of the shelves and managed to squeeze between the shelf and the wall. It was tight, and there was a musty smell that tickled my nose.

I held my breath, afraid to sneeze.

The door to the cairn room creaked and my pulse increased. The footsteps were still loud, reminding me of Rakshina's cadence of steps. She stopped moving, and I wondered if she could see me, or if she had decided no one was here.

She said a word that I didn't recognize as a rush of magic washed over me. It passed through my energy, completely ignoring me.

"Siekewa," she hissed, her voice echoing in the small space. "I know you are here."

The magic had been a finding spell. Drekvic's mark on me must have drawn her here, but her magic didn't recognize me as a siekewa, so I was ignored. I prayed that my luck would hold.

She said another word in her strange language and more magic was thrown into the room. The compulsion spell once again rushed passed me in my hiding spot.

I was starting to get light-headed from holding my breath, so I silently inhaled through my mouth, praying that it wouldn't make me cough. There was a tickle in my throat as I clenched my teeth.

"Damn, missed it again," Rakshina hissed.

Her loud steps were receding, but I heard her stop to scratch something on the wooden door. I listened until she had walked out of the cairn hall before breathing again. I waited awhile longer, not wanting her to come back.

Chester would be worried. I'd hurried away after leaving the ring, hoping to get to the cairn hall before he got back. I could just say that I'd gone to the restroom.

I'd have to think of something else, but I had to get out of the cairn hall first.

The door to the cairn room was now wide open, pressed into its hinges as Rakshina had written on it. There was a protection circle drawn on the door with a single character in the center. I didn't recognize it, and it didn't bother me as I slipped out of the room.

I was grateful I'd worn flats; the soft soles were silent as I carefully made my way outside. It was only one street over to blend back into the crowds, and I didn't see Rakshina anywhere.

I felt very small mixed in among the spirits. I knew how to get back to the garden, but my legs didn't seem to be working right and my heart was still loud in my ears. I managed to make it back to the garden in one piece and snatched up my ring from where I had hidden it. I let my power seep back into me and the lethargic feeling vanished. The guilt wasn't so easily dissipated, especially when I noticed the two steaming mugs sitting on the edge of the fountain.

I didn't want to go back into the crowd, but I

wasn't sure how Chester was going to find me again. He'd obviously noticed I was missing. I sat down on the edge of the fountain, deciding to wait.

Only a couple minutes passed before a green, glowing bird flew into the garden. It started chirping loudly, making me flinch. Chester was close behind it. When he saw me sitting next to our drinks, he hurried forward and reached out a hand, but didn't touch me. His shoulders slumped in relief and he put his hands on his hips.

"Where were you?" he demanded.

"I had to use the bathroom," I said, deciding I'd stick with my original lie. "I just got lost coming back."

"My bird couldn't find you. Your energy signature was gone." He gestured at the flying creature and it vanished in a pop of light.

I shrugged, unsure of how to answer that. "I came back as soon as I found the opening. I figured I'd wait for you to return."

"I was worried when I couldn't find you."

I smiled, trying not to make it look like it was breaking my cheeks.

"You worry too much. I'll wait for you next time, okay?" I turned to the glowing fountain and grabbed one of the cups he'd gotten us. The coffee was still hot with a hint of sugar and cream. It warmed me all the way to my toes, and I clutched it like a lifeline. I could only pray that Chester wouldn't notice the energy signature of the cairn in my bag.

I hardly paid attention as Chester told me there was one other thing I needed to see before we could leave and he began leading me through the crowd. My mind felt like it was shutting down so I wouldn't have to think about lying to my friend. I closed my eyes for a moment, taking a deep breath and steeling myself. I accepted what I had done and what I was going to do in the future. I didn't have to like it, but I had to do it, and nothing would change the fact that my little sister needed me.

Chester had taken my hand and was leading me toward the library. I could see the angel wings lit up with an inner light and I was curious about what he could show me that we hadn't already seen.

Once inside, we went directly to the crowded second floor. Several people were milling about in a large gallery of paintings. We had to leave our coffee by the door, but Chester assured me that they would be safe and untouched until our return. I took a deep gulp of mine before abandoning it.

"I thought you would like this since you have so many questions," he said, gesturing to the library. "It's the story of the first collectors. This festival is the anniversary of our creation."

"I saw this," I said, gesturing to the first painting. It was Fate and the god that she had shown me in her vision, holding hands as the world grew between them.

"That is Hope," Chester confirmed, gesturing to the male god beside Fate. Where Fate was golden and light, Hope was pale with dark hair and hazel eyes. He reminded me of Drekvic.

We moved on to the next painting, Chester standing just behind my shoulder to keep me from being jostled. Fate was holding a child, small and delicate and looking just like his father.

"They can't show it because Fate won't tell anyone how he did it, but the story goes that their son broke the world into different realities and that's how she and Hope were cursed apart."

"Cursed?" I looked up at him, brow furrowed. "Wait, he broke the world?"

"Yes, to both of those things," Chester said, chuckling slightly. "Their son was very powerful. When he was young, he wanted to play a trick on his family, so he took a portion of his father's power while he was sleeping."

"You can't take someone's power," I interrupted.

Chester raised an eyebrow at me and I shut my mouth. I wanted to hear the story, but it wouldn't happen if I kept interrupting him.

"With that extra power, he wanted to make a safe place where his family could live. Even with their status as gods, they were always wandering the earth, greeting people. Their son wanted a place to call home, so he planned to make one.

"Instead, he accidentally broke the realities. No, I don't know how he did it. Like I said, Fate won't share the information. By breaking the realities, he upset the balance of light and dark. He took light from your reality to create the Beyond, making it completely pure. The displaced energy of this broken balance broke off and opened up the spirit world.

"Because Hope's power was used to create the Beyond, he was pulled into that world and can't leave. Fate was dragged to the spirit world because even as a goddess, she's still technically a spirit. She can leave whenever she wants, but the moment she lets her guard down, she's dragged back. She can't go to the Beyond at all because she has darkness within her. Effectively, she is cursed to never be with Hope."

He gestured to the next painting. It showed Fate and Hope staring at each other through some sort of mirror, unable to touch or speak. Both were crying.

"This is where the collectors were created,"

Chester said, pulling me along in his history lesson to the next painting. "To alleviate the stress of a broken world, Fate decided to take the chaotic souls from your reality and bring them to the Beyond once their flesh ceased to live. By doing so, the evil in their bodies would vanish and their souls become purified in the Beyond."

The painting was of Fate throwing a glowing soul up into the sky, where Hope's hands were outstretched to receive it.

"She created the collectors because there were too many for her?" I asked.

"Yes. She was getting overwhelmed, especially because she couldn't go to the Beyond herself. She couldn't be sure the souls got there safely, only push them through the gates.

"So, one Winter Solstice, she used the latent power of the world to create the first collector. That's why we have this festival, to celebrate our founding and honor Fate for her sacrifice."

"But what happened to their son?" I asked, suspicion clawing at my chest.

"I think you know the answer to that," Chester replied, stopping me in front of another picture.

It was a man holding a ruby ring in his hand, looking extremely sad. Behind him, I could see the layers of each reality. He stood in my world, the spirit world floating just above, beautiful in its perfection. The Beyond was represented by the same distracting stars. When I studied the figure, my breath caught in my throat.

His mop of dark hair looked nothing like Fate's. The face was familiar, and his long black lashes were slightly lowered. My first impression was that he was bored, but the slump of his shoulders made me think otherwise.

"It's him," I whispered, unable to help myself.

"I thought so," Chester replied, looking away.

"He's Fate's son?" I asked, wanting to reach out and touch the child Drekvic's face. He was a boy once, immature and playing with powers he didn't understand.

"I think so."

I turned away from the painting, feeling sick. I suddenly understood Drekvic in a way that I rarely understood anyone. I walked to one of the benches lining the walls and sat down, feeling unreal as I stared at the tiled floor.

Chester sat down next to me.

"Are you okay?"

"No," I whispered. "All this time he's just been trying to find a way to bring his parents back together?"

"From what Fate has told me, he's trying to gather enough power to put the realities back together," Chester said, taking my hand and rubbing the back of it with his thumb. "It's impossible. It's easier to break things than it is to put them back together."

"I'm just like him." My voice was soft, and I felt like I was going to faint. "I would do anything to save my family." I had to bite my lip to keep myself from telling him everything.

"No, Ellie, you're not," Chester said, standing up and kneeling in front of me. His grip changed, but he never let go of my hand.

He forced me to look at him, his lustrous brown eyes intense with his conviction. "He gave up his humanity. He's obsessed. He's had thousands of years to let this go, to find a better way, but he keeps using others and torturing them in order to get more. He will never have enough power, Ellie. He knows it, but he keeps doing it anyway."

"I've spent my entire life trying to cure people of addiction because of my father. I've obsessed over it and struggled. I've ignored my sister. I didn't have any relationships with people because I didn't have time. I *know* what he's going through. To save family, to make them happy, I'd do anything."

"Ellie, listen to me," Chester said, reaching up and grabbing my arm. "You are not like him. Do you know what turned him into a siekewa?"

I shook my head, feeling tears rising in my eyes. I didn't believe him, and I was afraid. No matter what Chester told me, I would still give the stone to Drekvic to save Jana.

"His hatred of himself. He felt responsible for tearing his family apart even though he was a child and it was a mistake. He's punished himself enough, Ellie, but he still hates himself. That hatred, over thousands of years, turned him into a siekewa. That's how he creates others. You don't hate yourself nearly enough because what happened to your father and what happened to your sister was *not your fault*."

He ran his hands along my cheeks, wiping away my tears.

"What if I can still fix it?"

"Your sister and your father are dead."

"But my mom isn't," I said, wishing I could tell him everything so he would understand my hope.

"I'll find a way to get you home," he promised, smiling.

I gave him a small smile in return and nodded. He pulled me forward slightly, giving me a quick hug before standing. I let him go, leaning back on the bench and composing myself.

My father was long gone, destroyed by his lust for power. My sister was lost in limbo, but I could still reach her. I could still save her, and I wouldn't let my friendship with Chester stop me. Once I called Drekvic, he would release Jana's soul.

I'd worry about whatever chaos I created later.

CHAPTER TEN

The sun was shining into my window, bathing me in a golden glow and painting my closed eyelids red. I was tangled in my blanket, one foot wrapped up like a burrito while the other lay on top. I hadn't bothered to change out of my black dress, and the skirt was tangled in the blanket was making it difficult to escape. When I was finally free, I stood up, unsteady on my feet.

The emotions of the previous night had left me feeling raw and vulnerable. I pushed away the heaviness, remembering that Drekvic had been a child once. He had a family and he had lost them, just like me. He just wanted to put his world back together, and I wanted to save an important piece of mine.

Our obsessions matched, and I bit my lip, worried. If I was like Drekvic, did that mean I would become as scary as him? I sighed, sitting back down on the bed and rubbing my temples. I felt like I hadn't slept at all, and chills ran down my arms as I thought about what might happen.

I knew Drekvic could come to me in Chester's house. Chester wouldn't check on me unless he heard us talking or if I shouted. I could do this and be done before Chester found out anything. Jana was almost free.

Would she be proud of me? I wondered as I stood up again and walked to the bathroom, planning on taking a shower. Jana wouldn't give the cairn to Drekvic in order to save herself. Would she be mad that I was doing it to save her?

I pushed those worries out of my head as the warm water of the shower hit my face. No matter what happened, I wasn't going to let him keep her.

The quick shower washed away the rest of my melancholy and I got dressed in a plain t-shirt and jeans. Feeling more normal than I had in weeks, I sat on the floor and pulled out the velvet bag with the cairn from my purse.

Once I gave Drekvic his stone, our bargain would be complete and he would give me Jana's soul. I would be able to figure out how to get her to the Beyond. I could ask Chester. Then all I'd have to do was figure out how to get home.

The cairns held a lot of power. I could sense it even through the bag. If Drekvic was planning on misusing that power, I'd have to do something about it, but Jana came first. I'd fix whatever I broke after she was safe.

I took a deep breath, smelling the faint dusty scent of the guest room. I relaxed my shoulders and found the calm center in all the chaos inside me. I wrapped myself in my magic, protecting my heart and mind from intrusion.

When I was ready, I took another deep breath and whispered the siekewa's name.

He appeared, just as he had before. He saw me sitting in the middle of the room and looked immediately concerned.

"Did you fall down?" he asked, his voice sickly sweet.

I stood up, brushing a hand across the back of my jeans to get rid of any clinging dirt. Drekvic looked good, as he always did. His blue eyes still seemed dangerous and all-knowing, but even as I met his gaze, I wasn't afraid of him anymore.

"You don't scare me," I said, not really thinking about what was coming out of my mouth. I had the upper hand in this conversation, and I had questions.

"That's good," he replied, moving forward.

I held my hand up, pushing against his chest to stop him from coming closer. He raised an eyebrow and allowed the distance to stay between us when I dropped my hand. His magic was still overwhelming, but I was prepared this time, and I didn't collapse in a drunken heap.

"Why do you want the cairn?" I asked, my voice steady and low. I didn't want Chester to overhear us.

"I told you, it's pretty."

"Any good relationship is built on trust. If you lie to me about this, how can I believe you aren't lying to me about other things?" I crossed my arms and cocked my hip.

"We're in a relationship now? When did that happen?" He asked, a crooked smile appearing at the corners of his mouth.

"We're building one," I replied, tapping my fingers on my elbow. "Why do you want the cairn?"

Drekvic didn't answer right away. He studied me, his blue eyes narrowed in distrust. I lifted my chin, unwilling to look away first. A twinge of pleasure shot through me when he rolled his eyes and glanced at the door.

"Without it, I might never achieve my goals," he

replied, looking back shrugging like it wasn't important.

"What's your plan?"

"Oh please, Ellie. You can't expect me to trust you completely when the last time I saw you, you tried to kill me with a blast of raw power. A man has to keep some air of mystery."

"You're Fate's son," I said, hoping to shock some truth out of him. "Your mistake broke your family apart, and now you're trying to fix it."

He laughed at that, too loud. I glanced at the door, listening for any sign of Chester, but I didn't hear anything. It was still early he was probably was still asleep.

"My family abandoned me. Why would I try to fix something that let me down?" he demanded, his voice brimming with disgust.

I recognized the burning fire in his emotions. It was how I'd felt when my father had burned himself by overdosing on stored magic. His brain couldn't keep him alive once the magic had fried it. The doctors said he would never recover, and he never did. I had gone a little crazy myself, diving into research and projects to study addiction. I couldn't fix my own family, but I had sworn my work would help others. Drekvic had that same drive.

"Because you loved them," I said, keeping my voice even.

"Was there something you wanted from me or did you just want to see my pretty face?" he asked, changing the subject and putting a few more paces between us as he prepared to leave.

"I want my sister," I demanded, stepping forward and closing the distance between us.

"You remember our bargain," Drekvic said,

already dismissing me.

"I remember," I replied, uncrossing my arms and revealing the velvet pouch hidden in my hand.

Disbelief and hope flickered across his face, vanishing almost as quickly as they appeared.

"Give me Jana first," I demanded, holding out my other hand.

Drekvic pulled a glowing vial from his pocket and held it up. "You'd better not be trying to trick me," he demanded, tossing Jana's vial to me lightly.

His throw was short, and I lunged forward, hitting my knee on the wooden floor. Pain blossomed through my leg, but my fingers wrapped around the smooth vial.

Relief fluttered through me, so strong that I didn't realize I'd dropped the velvet pouch until I heard Drekvic near my ear, his clothes rustling as he stooped to pick it up.

I scrambled back away from him, the pain in my knee fighting back in protest. I clutched Jana to me as I scooted across the floor until my back hit the wall, watching as Drekvic opened the velvet pouch.

He tipped it over, dropping the white stone into his palm. There was a brilliant flash of light as the cairn hit his skin, but it faded quickly, and then he was just standing there, entranced by the power rolling off of it.

"I never could steal Fate's magic," he whispered, "but I guess I never needed to. She was planning on giving me a piece of it all along."

He started laughing, and I had a sinking feeling in my chest that told me I might have done something I couldn't fix. I pulled on my sapphire ring as Drekvic's power started to fill the room, threatening to choke me with its thick, ashy texture.

I wasn't surprised when the power drew Chester

into the room, his sword drawn and his face worried. He was wearing a t-shirt and sleeping shorts, his dark hair messy and bed lines on his face.

His eyes met mine across the room, making sure I was still in one piece. He looked back at Drekvic, his grip tightening on the sword. Horror passed over his face as he realized what the siekewa was holding.

Drekvic was still laughing, and I clutched Jana closer to me, careful not to crush her. I had saved Jana, but my struggles were really just beginning.

"I'll see you again, Ellie," Drekvic whispered. His silky voice echoed throughout the room and gave me chills. I pulled my feet underneath me, ready to run if I needed to, but Drekvic vanished, popping out of the room as though he'd never been there at all.

As his power disappeared, I dropped back down on the floor, breathing heavily. I had done it. Jana was safe.

Chester hurried over to me, kneeling down in front of me.

"What did you do?" he demanded, his voice wavering slightly.

With a trembling hand, I held out Jana's soul to him.

"I saved my sister." Even to me, my voice sounded small.

"He took your sister?" Chester took the vial reverently, a look of grief flowing across his face. "So you gave him a cairn to get her back. That's why you came to the spirit world?"

"Yes."

I wanted to tell him I was sorry, that I didn't realize how powerful it would make Drekvic, but I couldn't lie to him. I didn't like the outcome, but I wasn't sorry, and would do it again if I had to.

Chester sat down next to me, leaning against the wall, looking haggard and pale. I reached out to touch his hand, and his skin was cool.

"What will he do with the stone?"

"The cairns allow us to collect souls without their permission. Some souls struggle even when it's their time to go. We're able to remove them from their bodies, and the cairn's magic keeps them calm while we take them through the gates. Some will still struggle, but we can focus on opening the gates while our cairn focuses on the soul. If he's using the cairn, he can just take the souls without a bargain. He doesn't need to grant wishes in return for payment. He can just take them."

I held out my hand for Jana's soul, afraid. He gave her back to me and I cradled her with both hands.

"He wants to put the world back together so there's only one reality? Then Fate and Hope don't have to be separated?" I asked, wondering if I had gotten the entire story right.

"He can't," Chester replied, his voice soft.

"Why not? If he has enough power…"

"The Beyond is a sacred place. Without it, there would be too many souls, thousands would be lost and unclaimed. Your world would fall apart as the creatures that live here in the spirit world overpowered it. Maybe Drekvic made a mistake when he broke the world into different realities by not balancing each one appropriately, but if he hadn't done it, I think Fate and Hope would have themselves, eventually."

He ran a hand through his hair, taking a deep breath. The color was returning to his face, and he nodded as though he was thinking about something.

"Fate wouldn't want this. She'd want to stop him, otherwise chaos would take over," I said, trying to find reassurance.

"I don't know what Fate would want," Chester replied. "She must have known all this would happen. Why else would she force you to stay here in the spirit world? Why else would she have stopped to talk to me me the last night and kept me from returning to you right away? I'm guessing that's when you got the cairn."

I nodded, the puzzle starting to fall together. I ran my fingers along the stopper on Jana's vial. I was afraid to open it, because I didn't want her to be let loose here. I had to get to the Beyond somehow, but I also had to clean up the mess I'd made. There was no point taking Jana to the Beyond if I allowed Drekvic to put the worlds back together.

"She guided him to Jana, somehow," I thought, feeling anger and hurt.

I stood up, determined.

"I need to talk to Fate." I held a hand out to help him up.

He took it and I pulled him to his feet. He narrowed his eyes at me and asked, "Why?"

"I need to talk to her about how to stop the siekewa. Also, I think I need a cairn."

"You want to become a collector?"

"Not really, but it's the only way I can think of to stop him. I'll do what I have to." I headed towards the closet and asked for sneakers and socks.

"No," he said, his voice pained. I looked behind me to see Chester's hunched shoulders and down-turned gaze.

"I can't sit here and do nothing," I insisted.

"Let's talk to Fate first, then you can decide. Maybe she can just take care of it," he pleaded.

I already had a feeling that Fate had set the entire

thing up for this moment. I didn't know what she had in store, but I was certain that she'd led me here. She wouldn't turn me from my path now, regardless of Chester's hopes. Looking into his dark eyes and realizing that I'd already betrayed his trust once, I would give him a moment for hope.

"I'll wait until we talk to Fate before I make a decision," I said.

He nodded, leaving the room to get dressed. He came back quickly, wearing his usual dark clothes and leather vest. I stepped into him as he wrapped his arm around my waist and he used his power to teleport us to the library.

As we walked through the elaborate room, I tried to focus on my path. It would be easy to let someone else deal with Drekvic, but I couldn't risk it. If he managed to pull the Beyond and the spirit world to my reality, then Jana would never be able to rest. My mother would be in danger, too, and that was unacceptable. Once I found out what Fate had planned, I would commit to stopping Drekvic, but I needed to know what I was getting into first.

Fate was in her office, plotting something out on her large desk. When she looked up at the opening elevator and saw us, she started laughing.

It all clicked together. When I had first met Fate, she had already assigned Chester to watch my soul. She had known that I would make it here to the spirit world, and she had to of known my goal. She'd led me to Melo, the same person that connected Jana to Drekvic. She distracted Chester when I went to steal the cairn. She'd set me up, for something, and she'd put my poor sister in the crossfire.

My muscles tensed and I felt my heart-rate increase as rage blurred the edges of my vision. She had done this to Jana and to me, and I hated her. I stalked forward, my hair floating in the energy I was angrily pulling from my sapphire.

"How *dare* you," I hissed, unable to hide the venom in my voice. "You pushed Jana into making that deal. You manipulated me into coming here and trying to save her. You knew I would do exactly what you wanted!"

"Oh Ellie, of course I did," Fate replied, standing up and walking around her desk. I didn't want her to touch me, so I took a step back.

"Why?" I demanded, trying to control the building desire to strike out.

"I can only influence my son indirectly for so long," she replied, shrugging. "He's getting too close. I needed someone with the power to stop him before he succeeded." Her eyes were watery, and I was taken aback by the display of emotion.

"If all three realities merge, do you know what would happen?"

I shook my head, wanting her to elaborate.

"As you know, each soul goes to the Beyond to be cleansed. Then, if it chooses, it can go back to reality to be born again. Something like seventy percent of babies are reborn souls. If there is no cycle, no souls can be resurrected. They'd have nowhere to go, and the world would be haunted. Seventy percent of babies would be soulless, no better than plants."

My brain struggled to comprehend the gravity of that statement. Ghosts would be everywhere, causing random energy spikes and accidents as they tried to communicate with the living. Children without souls would go into a coma and die, with no will to live. The thought of sparks of life with no chance to survive made my heart throb.

Fate raised a hand to rub her temple, her beautiful face a perfect mask of pain and regret.

"I had to do something, so I looked for someone like you. You had to have a child, or at least a sibling."

I looked up at her in horror. If I hadn't had Jana, my future child would have been her victim. I was shaking so badly that I had to dig my nails into my palms to keep myself from lunging at her.

"You had to be able to see the siekewas and the collectors. I found you, messed up your childhood to get the personality I wanted, did what I had to do. I've made you perfect."

"And then you manipulated Jana into seeking out the siekewa." My voice rose in pitch as my control crumbled beneath my rage. "You took my sister away from me the same way you took my father. You would have taken my unborn child. What if I hadn't been willing to make a deal? What if I had walked away? You would have left Jana with him?" I sounded hysterical, and I could see Chester take a step closer to me, whether to comfort or stop me I wasn't sure.

"All souls will be saved eventually, so yes, I took that risk. It was that or let countless other people suffer."

"Our lives aren't yours to play with!" I shouted, draining my ring in one quick swipe and pulling the power into me. My emotion fueled it and I reveled in the purity of it.

Decisive in my outrage, I threw that power at Fate. I put absolutely everything I had into that charge, pushing away all the fury and agony that had filled my life since Jana died. I threw in all of my guilt for betraying Chester by giving the stone to Drekvic, all the hate I held for myself and for Fate along with it.

When the energy was gone, I collapsed to the

ground in a heap, sobbing. Chester knelt down next to me, pulling me into his arms and stroking my hair as I cried into his chest.

I felt Fate kneel down as well, unable to see her through my tears and Chester's arms. Her hand touched my wrist and my power slowly seeped back into me. She must have caught it to give it back. She knew I still needed it.

CHAPTER ELEVEN

Chester held me until my sobbing subsided. I was exhausted and more than a little embarrassed. Fate gave me a handkerchief from her desk, and I wiped my face. When I finally stood up from my undignified heap on the ground, I was calmer, but I felt spent. I had never tried to kill someone with my magic before, and the amount of power I was able to channel at once surprised me. I hadn't realized I could hold so much. I felt a new respect for my sapphire ring.

Fate had still caught the assault as though it was nothing. She had returned it to me gently, and even though I needed her, I still wanted to kill her. I watched as she settled behind her desk and gestured to the empty chairs in front of it. I glanced at Chester, who looked uncomfortable and worried, still standing near the elevator.

He nodded and moved with me to sit down.

"Ellie, can I count on you to stop my son?" Fate asked, her voice calm and gentle.

I met her gaze, feeling numb. I didn't care that she had done what she had to do to save the world. I still hated her. She had destroyed *my* world, and she wasn't even sorry for my loss. I pulled my bag into my lap and griped it tightly, thinking of Jana's soul inside. I had what I needed. Chester would help bring Jana to the Beyond, and that would be that.

I didn't have to stop Drekvic at all, but I was going to.

I sighed, my breath hitching slightly at the end. "I have to become a collector, don't I?"

"It's the only way for you to grow powerful enough to stop him," Fate agreed.

"Just walk away, Ellie," Chester said, his determined gaze never looking away from Fate. "The collectors will stop Drekvic. He can't be stronger than all of us. You have no reason to change."

"I have two reasons," I said, touching his hand in a plea to get him to look at me. He didn't. "What will you do when Drekvic takes your soul? Who will save *you*?"

Chester stood up, pulling away from me and making fists. "You don't understand the choice you're making. You're giving up everything, your entire life. Your mother will never know what happened to you. Everyone will mourn you as if you'd died, and you'll never be able to have a family, a life. You don't want this!"

"Chester, tell Ellie why you became a collector," Fate ordered gently.

The blood drained from his face. He looked defeated as he sat back down and slouched in the chair. He wouldn't look at me, and his voice sounded a thousand years away.

"I became a collector because of Michael," he started, pausing and swallowing loudly.

I waited until he was ready to continue, barely breathing.

"I was married when I was eighteen; it wasn't so

strange in that time. My wife, Alice, got pregnant almost immediately. Michael was born when I was just nineteen. He was my whole world."

I remembered Chester talking about the children collectors, his shoulders stiff and his voice soft. My question had brought up memories of his past, and then I had tried to pry even further by asking him why he became a collector. I really didn't think I was going to like this story, and my hands tightened into fists on my lap.

"For his fifth birthday, I bought him a pony. It was an old and fat thing, perfect for him to learn how to ride." Chester stopped again, taking a deep breath.

"You don't have to tell me," I said.

"Yes, he does," Fate said, and I glared at her.

"Why? To fulfill your own sadism?" I snarled.

"You need to understand your choice before you make it," she snapped back. "I need you to understand what you are giving up before I can trust you."

"It's okay, Ellie," Chester said, his voice quiet. I turned back to him and reached out to take his hand. He gave my fingers a reassuring squeeze and continued.

"Like I said, the pony was old and fat. I didn't think I'd need to worry about Michael getting hurt. Something spooked the stupid thing and it broke away from its lead with Michael on its back. It tried to jump the fence..." His voice trailed off, his brown eyes seeing the scene all over again.

"It didn't make it. It hit the wood and fell. Michael fell, too. He broke his neck. There was no collector for his soul."

"You could see them, too?" I asked, unable to help myself.

"Yes. I knew that Michael's death was an accident.

115

He was going to become a lost soul. I—I couldn't let it happen." His eyes were wet with unshed tears. "When I confronted them, they said there was no hope for my son. He would become a ghost and there was nothing that could be done to save him. I refused to believe it. I insisted that I was his father, that *I* could save him. They had to show me how to help."

"Samuel is the oldest collector, the first one Fate created." He looked up at her, his jaw squared and his gaze cold. "He took pity on me and brought me to her."

Fate stared back at him, her expression unapologetic.

"She told me that I couldn't save my son, but that she would give me a chance to try. She said I would never die, that I could try as often as I pleased, but she promised that I wouldn't be able to take him to the Beyond."

He looked away from Fate and rubbed the back of his neck with his free hand. I still held the other, my fingers curled tightly around his, wishing I could do more.

"I went to where his soul was and he couldn't see me. He was calling for me, but I couldn't reach him." His voice broke and he closed his eyes, taking a deep breath. "Alice couldn't see me, either. The authorities told her I was missing, and she had our second child alone. She died shortly after and my daughter grew up without parents."

I stood up and put an arm around him. He was still sitting, but he leaned into my stomach, eyes closed. His arm went around my waist, clinging to me as though I was a lifeline. I stroked his silky hair, my heart aching for his pain. I didn't know what to say.

"There is always another way, Ellie. I'd give

116

anything to undo my choice. I don't think you should do this."

"I'm sorry," I whispered, my throat constricting. I couldn't see any other choice, especially now.

I looked up at Fate, my arm still around Chester's shoulders. "I don't trust you," I told her frankly, "but all my choices suck. At least this way I can make a difference instead of just spending the rest of my life stuck here. My mom—she's never going to know what happened to me, but I can protect her from Drekvic's plans."

Fate nodded, a smug smile at the corner of her lips.

"I need a powerful cairn that can collect ghosts," I said, glad I was able to speak without my voice wavering. I didn't know what Jana's soul would be considered, but if she was a lost one, I had to be able to save her.

"There isn't such a cairn," Fate replied, brow furrowing. She crossed her arms and leaned back in her chair.

"You said that all souls will be saved eventually. If that's true, there must be a way to collect them you haven't told us about. Tell me."

Chester looked up at that, hope and anger waring for the dominance on his face.

"There is no such cairn!" Fate snapped, slapping her hands on the desk and rising halfway off her chair.

I flinched back, my arm falling from Chester as I brushed my magic. She still had the ability to scare me.

"The power isn't in the cairn but in the collector. You can see the spirit world and interact with ghosts. You will be able to save them. *You* are the person I've been waiting for to take my place so I can be with Hope in the Beyond."

A ripple of fear ran up my spine. I was going to take Fate's place?

She opened the top drawer of her desk and pulled out a ring.

The band was platinum with a simple vine pattern etched into it. The place setting held a small cairn and reminded me of the ones in Fate's hair. Even though smaller and more delicate that Chester's stone, it was radiating power that I could feel even across the desk.

"This cairn contains a large portion of my power," she said. "It will bond with your magic and make you more than what you are. It will keep you safe and guide you when you lose sight of your purpose."

She held it out to me. I glanced at Chester's unhappy face, hoping for his support before I took it. He looked like he wanted to stop me, but eventually he gave a small nod.

"Whatever you decide to do, I'll follow you," he told me.

I gave him an appreciative smile, and turned back to Fate.

"Chester told me that because you are a spirit you are constantly dragged back here to the spirit world. Will this change what I am?" I asked, wanting to know, but realizing that it wouldn't change my choice.

"Collectors are not spirits," Fate replied. "You will not become one either. As a collector, you will be able to traverse all the planes, and as long as you do not become too distorted by darkness, you will be able to reach the Beyond as well."

"How does this allow you to be with Hope?"

"I can die," she said. "Once my body dies, I can become a soul. If I am a soul, I am no longer a spirit and I can be with him." Her voice was so full of hope and desire that I believed her.

I reached out and took the ring. The band was warm from Fate's skin, and perfectly smooth. I slid it onto the middle finger of my right hand. It glistened next to my sapphire and I blinked away the sudden brightness.

I flinched as I realized I was standing in an all white space. There were no walls, nothing in the distance except for the whiteness. I squinted, trying to orient myself. When I turned, a woman was standing there, hands hidden in the folds of her white robes.

Her skin was a lovely cream color, mostly hidden by floor-length robes. Silver hair fell in a loose braid all the way to her ankles, curling lightly around her heart-shaped face. Long lashes accented her pale gray eyes. Despite having never seen her before, I knew her immediately.

This was the cairn's soul; Fate's created doppelganger, changed by the power of being trapped in the cairn.

"What power do you ask of me?" she queried. Her clear voice resonated inside my chest.

"Fate told me I had my own power. I shouldn't need yours," I replied.

"Fate tells many pretty stories," the soul replied, turning to look up into the white sky. I wondered what she could see that I couldn't.

"There's a siekewa stealing souls. I helped make it easier for him. I was hoping you could help me stop him," I explained.

She turned back to me, scowling. "You are the one she's been babbling about? Fate called you across the planes to give the siekewa a cairn. Did you save your sister?"

"I have her soul. I should be able to restore her to the Beyond. I think I can save all the wandering souls too."

"That is a large commitment."

"I won't let you run out of power. I have enough to keep us whole." I wasn't sure why I said it like that, but something about this soul made me want to protect her.

She walked toward me, studying me carefully.

"I want to be free of this place. I am tired of seeing the world through another's eyes."

"Once I stop the siekewa, I will set you free. I'll take you to the Beyond if you want."

"Truly?" she asked, her voice painfully hopeful.

"I promise."

She hugged me, and her touch was light as gossamer. Her hope and desire filled me, and I knew that no matter what happened I'd do whatever it took to keep my promise to her.

When she released me, I was back in front of Fate with Chester beside me. I wasn't alone in my head anymore. I could feel my cairn's spirit, curled up next to my soul, using my eyes as her own. She was curious, and seemed to be picking through my memories and trying to judge my character. It was distracting, but I found I could separate my thoughts from hers if I tried.

I looked up at Fate, noticing the faint lines around her eyes and creases around her tired smile for the first time. I wonder how long she'd lived with a second soul inside of her.

"I have waited so long to be free of that burden," she whispered, her voice full of emotion. "I can finally be with my dear Hope."

"How will I find you if I need your help?" I asked. Once she realized she could visit her lover and come and go as she pleased, I was confident Fate would be

120

all over the place.

"If you come into this room and call me, I will always come," she replied, standing up and running a hand through her hair. I nodded and stood up as well, turning toward the elevator door.

"Ellie?" she called, making me look back at her. "Thank you."

I considered cursing at her, but instead clenched my jaw closed. I wasn't doing this for her.

She smiled, looking young again. She nodded and spun in a circle, vanishing like a puff of smoke.

CHAPTER TWELVE

"You're not even trying," Chester admonished. I jumped, looking away from the lake and focusing on him. He wasn't really upset, but after hours of practice my mind was starting to wander more than I'd like to admit.

We were sitting on the grass, cross-legged in front of each other in the meadow where we first met. He had taken his necklace off and his cairn was sitting in his palm, glittering in the light. I kept my cairn facing the light as well, as Chester explained that light was important when it came to cairns. They would glow if it was dark, expending valuable power needlessly. Cairns were the soul's true guide and they always wanted to be visible.

Each cairn was unique, as Fate took lost and discarded souls from the spirit world and gave them a home. The collectors were hand-picked to be guides, but the cairns were meant to be pure power. As long as a soul still had energy, it was given a new purpose and a place to belong.

I couldn't help but draw a comparison to the siekewa and Drekvic using souls as power. The souls Fate picked wanted to be chosen and were happy to help her, but Drekvic's souls were coerced into service. Their power was not freely given and would always be incomplete.

The cairn Fate gave me was different, a part of Fate herself, and had lived apart from her long enough to become her own soul. It was disturbing to think about, but I imagined it was how new souls were created. If a baby was conceived and a soul never arrived, its mother would subconsciously fill it with her own, and when they were separated by birth, the baby's soul would develop on its own. I wondered if Fate's prediction of soulless children would bear fruit, but it was too scary of a possibility to let happen regardless.

Drekvic had a cairn, so I had to stop him, no matter what.

"Reach for the power again," Chester said.

I took a deep breath and stretched my awareness to the cairn on my finger. The power flowed into me, as it always did. The magic was always a rush. It was so clean that it tended to wash away all the thoughts in my head and made me want to keep pulling, even though I had all I needed. I wondered if this was the rush my father was always searching for.

"Focus, Ellie," Chester said sternly.

I turned my thoughts back to the task at hand.

With a gentle touch, I brushed Chester's mind, trying to reach out to his soul. I wasn't trying to take it yet, but I needed to know what they felt like before I could do anything. I had my eyes closed, but I could feel him flinch as my power reached him. Perhaps my touch wasn't as delicate as I wanted it to be.

"You're too controlling," he cautioned. His voice sounded pained, and I felt even worse.

As I'd learned time and again over the course of

the morning, hesitation was my worst enemy. Chester's mind automatically threw up barriers to keep me out, and instead of gently soothing him, I overreacted and pushed. Chester grunted and shoved back with his own power. I fell back onto the grass with open eyes, feeling as though I'd been mentally burned.

I sighed, frustrated. I knew what worked for Chester in greeting a new soul wasn't going to work for me. Despite our first meeting where he wanted to strangle me, I'd discovered that he was a gentle man, with magic softer than silk.

My touch was sharp and precise, like a needle. Souls didn't like that. I had to be able to coax them out of their barriers instead of taking them by force, and the trauma had a way of making them panic. It could make them too upset to collect, eventually losing the ability to see the collectors at all. They would become lost.

"I'm sorry," I told Chester, sitting back up and crossing my arms over my legs. "I don't think I'm any good at this type of magic."

He looked at me, frustration written all across his face.

"That's not true at all," he said. "I am making it difficult for you because you are going to be fighting someone that won't allow you to collect him, so you have to coax him without him realizing until it's too late. That's why we're doing this exercise."

"I don't know how to coax!"

"Yes, you do. You know how to make things do what you want. Remember that basket game you played at the carnival? Your ball was so eager to do what you wanted that it broke the basket. The goal is to make them do what you want them to on their own."

I thought about the festival and how the ball had shot toward the basket like a bullet. It happened because I had remembered Jana's words and *asked* it to move. Maybe souls were like that, too. They just needed to be asked nicely.

"Let me try again," I said, feeling a sliver of hope.

He nodded, rolling his shoulders to relax himself. I did the same, taking a deep breath and reaching back to the cairn. I let the power fill me until I had a firm grip on it.

Instead of reaching out to Chester, I asked the power to create a bubble around us, flowing like a gentle stream at my request. I could feel Chester's soul inside my bubble. It shimmered with a bright, golden light. I could feel his strength and the sense of justice that defined him so firmly. I asked my magic to fill the bubble and press against his mind.

This time he didn't flinch, and I felt his gentle sigh of relief.

Could you come with me, please? I asked his soul, and to my immense surprise, it unwound from his body and curled up in my outstretched hands. I hadn't even realized I had moved, but I was holding Chester's soul, and it was beautiful.

His warmth and vitality were overwhelming. I understood, in that moment, what it was to be a collector, what it meant to protect these souls and give them a chance to reach the Beyond. I wanted to hold Chester's soul and protect it, but my cairn was talking to me.

He's not ready to go, she said, insistently tapping against my thoughts. *Put him back before his body shuts down.*

I nodded, asking the soul to return to Chester's

body. I opened my eyes and saw him take a deep, relieved breath. He opened his own eyes and smiled at me.

"That was beautiful, Ellie," he said, his eyes dancing. I pulled my power back and let it flow back into the cairn.

"That was amazing!" I jumped to my feet, feeling energized. I could do this. I knew exactly how to stop Drekvic. I'd just have to get close enough to make my move.

I looked out over the water, putting my hands on my hips. I would need help, but it wasn't impossible. The collectors would have to be there to guide all of Drekvic's stolen souls back where they were meant to be.

I turned back to Chester, feeling hopeful.

"We can do this."

"I know we can," he replied, standing up and brushing the grass off his leather pants. "You're going to need more practice, but I don't think you can do it on me anymore."

I looked at him, confused and almost hurt.

"Ellie, I let you take my soul. If you had wanted to, you could have taken me anywhere and I wouldn't have tried to stop you. It's terrifying, to trust someone so much," he said, shrugging and seeming embarrassed. "You need someone who'll fight you, harder than I can, because no matter how much Drekvic wants you, I don't think he'll go quietly."

"Chester," I said, stepping closer to him and taking one of his hands. "I would never, ever hurt you *or* your soul." I remembered the feeling of his soul in my hands, knowing I had the power to do whatever I wanted with it, and shuddered at the thought that I could have hurt him.

"I know you won't, but you need a soul willing to put up a fight." He smiled and my heart stuttered. "My soul isn't willing to hurt you, and if he fights you, none of this practice will have mattered."

I nodded, feeling nervous about practicing with another person.

"Who do you suggest?"

"Rakshina."

CHAPTER THIRTEEN

Rakshina's home was out of place in the collector's city. She lived on the outskirts near a large forest that seemed to radiate mystery. The two-story house was a combination of black-painted stone and obsidian accents, without a crystal to be seen. It was modern looking, with a single slanted roof and lots of windows tinted so dark that I couldn't see through them. The equally black porch held only an old red rocking chair.

That was where we found her, drinking coffee from an over-sized mug. She looked unimpressed as Chester and I approached, but I could see a slight widening in the corner of her slanted eyes. She was looking at me, worry creeping into her silent stare. She stood up before we could walk up the front steps and Chester stopped in front of me.

"You are free of your bargain," she said to me. "You are now here to learn what must be done to stop my old friend now that he has his cairn, yes?"

"I know how to stop him," I replied, pushing past Chester to confront the siekewa myself. Her pale skin and dark hair intimidated me, reminding me of Drekvic, but I wasn't about to back down now. "I need to learn how to collect unwilling souls."

She looked up at Chester. "And you think I'm the most difficult person you know?" she asked, laughing a rich and melodious laugh.

"You know why I came here," Chester snarled, crossing his arms. He was clearly unhappy we needed Rakshina's help. "Siekewas are resistant to our powers naturally. She can take my soul with no problem, and I don't want her to battle with Drekvic to be the first time she comes up against a difficult soul."

"At least you are smart about some things. Come in," she said, turning to her ebony door and opening it for us.

I led the way, letting Chester guard my back.

Rakshina directed us to her large living room. The inside was just as dark as the outside, calling great attention to the grand windows that stretched from floor to ceiling toward the back of the house and the view of the dark forest beyond. The room was very modern, with furniture designed for a specific look rather than for comfort. Books and newspapers were scattered across the clean glass of her coffee table. There were bookshelves covered with glass knick-knacks and old tomes with no titles. A silver knife in a glass case caught my eye. It seemed to twist as I looked at it, curling in on itself and begging me to touch it. I turned away. To the left, I could see the kitchen and dining room beyond.

Other than the messy coffee table, the entire space was immaculate. Rakshina moved forward and collected her papers, putting them on the counter that separated the living room and kitchen.

"Sit," she said, gesturing to the three-seater couch. I did so, not wanting to seem rude. Chester didn't sit, and didn't seem to care that he was hovering. It was obvious he didn't like being in the siekewa collector's personal space.

Rakshina ignored him and sat on the matching love seat across from me. She studied me for a moment before holding out her hand. She didn't ask for me to take it, but I knew what she was doing. She wanted me to trust her, and for me to do that, I'd need to know who she was. I hadn't seen Drekvic's past when he touched me, but perhaps he had been blocking my gift somehow.

I couldn't see the other collectors, but all of them had a ceremony that erased their past and made them something new. Looking into Rakshina's pale eyes, I had a feeling that wasn't the case with her.

I started drowning the moment I took her pale hand. Rakshina's past was not pleasant. She had hurt people, killed them and stolen their souls. She had made bad deals, and while she had never gone against her word, the fine print in the contracts cheated people out of their souls even if they had thought they had held up their end of the bargain. But she had also helped people. There were people she had loved, people she had made deals with them that could be honored by breathing. When she had killed the collector that tried to stop her, instead of taking his cairn and trying to garner more power, her deal with cairn was to take the collector's soul to the Beyond and take his place. She had taken all of her accumulated souls to the Beyond and let them go, freeing them from their slavery.

I pulled away from her, took a deep breath and shuddered.

"I have not yet atoned for my sins," she said, "but I will not hurt you now, or ever."

"I know," I replied, rubbing my arms, feeling cold. "Will you help me?"

"Yes, but I don't think you understand what you are getting yourself into."

"Then tell me."

She glanced at Chester, and I understood her unspoken words.

"Chester," I said, trying to sound soothing. "You can either sit down and relax, or go wait outside. It's hard to concentrate with you hovering like that."

He looked like he wanted to snarl at me, but instead he sat down and leaned back into the couch, his arms still crossed. His presence was still stifling, and his dislike of Rakshina seemed to fill the room.

"For the love of Fate," Rakshina muttered. "Ellie was trying to be nice. You need to get out. She cannot work through the energy disturbance you're causing here."

"I won't leave Ellie by herself with you," he replied, and visibly tried to calm his emotions.

"Go sit in the kitchen then," she said. I noticed her cairn was glowing slightly on her neck, channeling her emotions and keeping the siekewa in check.

He stood up, clearly unhappy, and went to the kitchen as directed. He found a stool at the counter and sat turned away from us, still listening, but at least we couldn't see him glaring. Rakshina sighed and rubbed her forehead, turning back to me.

"You are planning on using your new cairn to take the souls he has collected?" she asked me, ignoring Chester now that he was out of her easy sight. I noticed she didn't say Drekvic's name out loud.

"Yes," I replied, leaning forward slightly.

"He will still have plenty of power stored within him. If you want to stop him, you will have to take his soul, not just his powerhouses." Rakshina leaned back, thinking. "If you can get close to him, I think you could probably do it. I know he likes you."

"How do you know that?" I demanded, leaning back into the couch again. I didn't want to think about Drekvic's feelings for me.

"The deal he made with you was extremely light. He obviously wanted the stone, but made no stipulations, included no back-out clauses. This is unusual. You took Chester's soul without trouble?"

"Once I figured out how to do it, it was easy."

She nodded. "It will be harder to take a siekewa's soul. It is how he made us. We will fight, tooth and claw, doing whatever necessary to keep our bodies whole. I will not allow my soul to hurt you, but Drekvic will not make that distinction. You have to be strong enough to stun him and keep him from resisting."

"Chester said that if you tear a soul out, it becomes a ghost." I twisted my sapphire ring, hoping I was strong enough to keep Drekvic's soul in line without hurting him.

"You care about that monster's soul becoming a ghost?" Rakshina asked, surprised.

"I won't let his soul become a ghost. I know how it feels to have your family torn apart by power. I know what its like to feel alone, and to try to fix things, only to make them worse. He may have strayed from his original path, but I think all this time he's been trying to gather souls so he can fix the realities so his family can be together again. He doesn't know Fate has already been cut loose from her responsibilities. I don't think he'll believe me if I just tell him, but if I can take him to the Beyond, I can show him."

"Do you know how to get to the Beyond?"

"It's up in the sky," I replied, remembering the stars that called to me. I pushed a loose strand of hair behind my ear and looked down at my knees. Even knowing there was a roof between the sky and me, I didn't want to look up.

"We will have to teach you how to go there and back by yourself. Making the journey with a squirming soul will be even more difficult. If you can do it, I think you will succeed. First, though, I have to tell you that your own soul is immune to a siekewa's magic."

"Huh?" I jerked my head back up and sat up in my seat, taken off guard by her change of topic and stunned by her words.

"I've been trying to coax your soul to play with me since you walked into my house. It has not even acknowledged me. That will work in your favor if he tries to distract you from your mission."

I remembered Drekvic trying to curse me and how it couldn't quite get a hold on me. I hadn't been able to get it off, but it had failed in what it was trying to do, and Chester had time to pull it away.

"When you try to take my soul, you must be aware of my magic as well. A siekewa's magic is unfriendly, and it will be uncomfortable. You may be immune to my curses, but siekewa magic is not all I can throw at you. Some of it will just be raw power. Keep in mind that Drekvic is many centuries older than I am, and may have more tricks. Now, let's start," Rakshina said, sitting up straight and closing her eyes.

I did the same, reaching out to my cairn. Just like I did with Chester, I attempted to build a bubble around us. Rakshina's magic lashed out, shattering my concentration and forcing my cairn's power away. I could taste her hostility, but I couldn't let her back down. I knew she could sense what I was feeling, so I made myself confident and strong. I forced the bubble

Wayward Soul by L.D. Greenwood

to explode out around us, not giving Rakshina a chance to break it.

What she did instead was build a bubble around herself, effectively blocking me from even brushing her soul. It frustrated me, and I took too long thing about it. I flinched when she counterattacked, the force of her magic shattering my bubble again. I must have cried out, because when I opened my eyes, Chester had stood up and almost come out of the kitchen. Rakshina still had her eyes closed on the love seat, posture ramrod straight.

"I'm fine," I told him, and dove back into my magic.

I knew force wouldn't work. Rakshina could easily break the bubbles I made to keep her soul from escaping. She had reformed her own bubble around herself, and when I sent tendrils of power to test its strength, she absorbed them, making her stronger. I could stun her with magic if I threw something big enough at her, but Drekvic was stronger than me. Rakshina didn't collect souls anymore, but Drekvic did.

I decided to ignore Rakshina for a moment and swept across the room. With my eyes closed, using only the senses my magic gave me, I found several containers on Rakshina's bookshelves that had once held souls. They were gone, but their misery and sadness remained, almost like a shadow of themselves. If this was Drekvic, where would he keep his souls? He had kept Jana's soul with him in a bottle. Did he do that with all his souls, or did he have his own type of cairn room?

To pull power from them, they had to be on him. In all of our encounters, Jana's was the only vial I had seen. What if Drekvic kept his souls inside of himself?

Maybe he hadn't had time to transition Jana's soul.
How would he separate his soul from those he used? I
tried to remember details about him, and I saw the
ruby ring he always wore. Gemstones could store
massive amounts of power. If this was a gemstone
native to the spirit world, with all the excess magic
here, wouldn't it be able to hold much more power?
What if he could house all his souls there and discard
the ring when there was no power left in it?

Rakshina's cairn was different from her soul, but it
still housed a lot of her power. I checked her bubble
again. It was protecting her soul, but her cairn was still
easy to get to.

Allow me, I heard my own cairn whisper, and I
passed control of the power to her capable hands.
Without hesitation, I watched her deftly pull
Rakshina's cairn away from the siekewa. It was what I
had done with Chester's soul, a gentle request that
sounded like a sweet promise. Once it was away from
her, the main source of Rakshina's power collapsed.
Her soul panicked, and I felt dark laces of magic swirl
around me.

I quickly pulled the bubble around us again,
capturing her flailing soul in a safe place. Her power
hurt me where it struck. I could feel blows all around
me, pounding at my psyche. I pulled the bubble
tighter, strengthening it until I was certain I wouldn't
lose Rakshina.

"Rakshina," I whispered, unable to stop from
saying the words outloud. "Come to me, please." Even
I could hear the compulsion in my voice, the
resonating strength. It reminded me of Fate, and as I
quietly accepted that I really was her replacement, I
felt my own power bolster the command.

Rakshina's soul slid from her as delicately and as

easily as Chester's had. It rested in the palm of my
outstretched hand. My cairn let Rakshina's cairn swirl
around along my fingers as well, and the combined
beauty of the two side by side surprised me.
Rakshina's soul dark soul seemed to draw in light,
while her cairn was brilliantly white, dancing around
in happiness as it shielded Rakshina from the world.

I realized in that simple gesture that while
Rakshina had killed the cairn's original collector to
steal his stone, the cairn had forgiven her, and loved
her all the same. They had a relationship that I hadn't
seen with Chester's soul, because I had only tried to
steal one. I wondered, if I used the same tactic with
Drekvic, if the souls he took would try to attack him
instead. I couldn't hold them all; I'd need help.

I opened my eyes to see Rakshina slumped back
into her chair, her chest rising and falling gently. Her
cairn was black, empty of the soul that gave it light.
Gently, I blew Rakshina's soul back to her body,
allowing it to settle just like Chester's had. Her cairn
once again glowed with faint light. Rakshina sat up
and opened her eyes, looking at me like she had never
before seen me.

"How did you do that?" she whispered,
shuddering.

I looked over at Chester, who had moved from the
kitchen back into the living room and was hovering.
His mouth hung open as well, and he looked
extremely troubled.

"What do you mean?" I asked, confused.

"You took my cairn. You took the light and power
out of it. The connection cut off… it was—never
mind. Tell me how you did it" she demanded. She had
a hand cradled protectively around her cairn now. I
had scared her.

"I didn't do that," I replied, twirling my cairn's ring around my finger. "My cairn did it. She asked it nicely."

"I've never heard of anyone being able to do it. Many collectors have tried and failed. Your cairn's soul was able to take it?" Rakshina said, her voice sounding almost hoarse.

I stood up, suddenly uncomfortable under her scrutiny. My cairn sent a reassuring wave of power into me, letting me know I was safe and guarded.

"Your soul was too protected, so I took your power source. I gave my cairn control of our magic, she pulled your cairn's soul away, and then I caught you. We caught you. She was helping me."

"Your cairn is conscious?" Chester asked, his voice sounding almost strangled.

I looked at him, unconsciously balling my hands into fists.

"Of course she is. Isn't yours?"

"No," he replied, looking down. "The cairns are just power source, we can't communicate with them."

I'm not special, my cairn whispered to me. *Cairns are nothing more than ghosts with a purpose. Normal collectors cannot interact with ghosts, but since you can, you can hear me. They seem to be overreacting.*

"When you made your deal with the cairn, how did you communicate with it?" I asked, wondering how it was possible that the collectors couldn't hear the souls in their care, even if they were trapped in stone.

"It's a little different for everyone," Chester explained, "but usually there's some sort of room with the cairn's spirit inside. It tells us what it wants in exchange for the power, and as long as we provide that, it will give us that power. We never speak to the cairn again until it's time to put it away and exchange it for another. Then it tells us if we fulfilled the bargain."

"What happens if you don't?" I asked.

"We take its place," Rakshina answered, looking up at me. "It has never happened, but that's what we've been told."

I sat back down, feeling isolated. Could I free the cairns as well?

My cairn interjected again. *They don't all want to be free. Many of them feel blessed that they were chosen for service,* it reassured me. *Rakshina's would never leave her, and has been drawing power from her while she sleeps to maintain the strength to serve. He loves her.*

I nodded. It must have looked strange to Chester and Rakshina, but the lesson was important. I could hold Drekvic's soul, and somehow, take him to the Beyond.

CHAPTER FOURTEEN

I was nervous whenever I thought about having to reach the Beyond. I wasn't ready to give up on life, and my soul yearned for the Beyond so badly, I was afraid of getting lost. Chester promised me that it wouldn't happen, that my willpower was stronger than my soul's instincts, but even so, I was unsure. I had too much to do to get trapped there, but Jana's soul needed saving, and I was going to take her there.

Before Chester and I left Rakshina, she had told me how to calm Jana's soul to be safely released, as she had lots of practice from when she freed her own souls. I couldn't fail her now.

The first step toward the Beyond was, in theory, easy. Collectors took souls through seven gates to reach the Beyond. Those seven gates kept it safe from monsters in the spirit world, and kept living souls safe from vengeful ghosts in my realm. Three of those gates were between my reality and the spirit world, so I didn't have to worry about them. It was the other four that I needed to unlock.

Lucky me though, my cairn was also a key. It would allow me to unlock the doors and guide my charge through. Chester's plan was to guide me through himself as I focused on containing Drekvic's soul. Despite trusting his idea, he thought it would be best if I knew how to open the gates myself in case of an emergency.

Knowing Drekvic was out somewhere made it difficult to focus on my lesson. Rakshina told me he wouldn't be sitting idly by while I trained. He would be stealing souls—several of the collectors had gone missing already. Rakshina was convinced that Drekvic and his newfound powers were responsible and that he now held more than one cairn.

I would have to save them as well. It was so much pressure I thought I was going to explode, but I was the only one whose soul Drekvic couldn't steal. We made a deal; he promised he wouldn't take my soul unless I gave it to him, so I was safe.

Everyone I cared about was another story. All of them could be stolen without a second thought—all my students, my mother, even Rakshina and Chester. I looked up at him as we sat in his living room. He was clearing a space on the floor where we could practice. I'd barely known him for a week, but I already cared about him. He was a little rough around the edges, but he was also gentle and playful. He was a dedicated father, and I knew that it must be eating away at him every day that his son was lost.

"Chester," I said, grabbing his attention as he pushed his antique coffee table toward the wall. He paused looking up at me expectantly. "Thank you—for everything."

"Don't get all mushy on me," he complained, pushing his table the rest of the way. "We have a lot to do before you get to have your moment."

"I need to tell you now, though, in case I can't do it," I insisted, walking over and getting in his way.

Disapproval took over his face, and I couldn't help but smile at his annoyance.

"I'm listening."

"That was all I really wanted to say," I replied, trying to hide my smile.

"You're welcome," he grumbled, turning away and grabbing a blanket from the couch to spread across the now vacant hardwood floor.

I grabbed the other end, helping him spread it across the space. When it was done, he grabbed some pillows and dropped them down as well, wanting to make it comfortable for us to concentrate. Once I was able to reach the gates, my body would go there as well, but apparently learning to transport myself was going to take some time.

"Where will I live once I stop him?" I wondered, thinking of Drekvic and trying to ease the tension. Chester was obviously concerned and I didn't want to start practicing if my teacher was annoyed.

"You can live wherever you want. You could even take Fate's old home. She's not using it anymore."

"Will you come house shopping with me?"

"Ellie, what are you doing? This is serious!"

I sobered, feeling his reprimand like a slap. I knew it was serious. I knew it would be dangerous. I had to be strong enough to handle it, but I also knew that I wouldn't give up. I *had* to succeed because I wanted Drekvic to know that he was loved and that his family was together again.

I also needed to reach the Beyond, because I couldn't save Jana's soul otherwise. I could let Rakshina do it, but I didn't trust her to treasure Jana like she should. She didn't know my sister, and I couldn't imagine Jana blindly trusting someone that looked so much like Drekvic. It had to be someone she knew, and that left only me.

"I could die," I said softly, looking up at him. "I don't want to think about it. I want to plan for the future, even if I never see it."

Chester walked over to me and put a hand on my shoulder.

"You're right. You could always live here. I've always wanted a roommate."

"Really? Normal people don't want roommates."

"Well, maybe not always. I wouldn't mind you as a roommate, but you'd have to cook for yourself."

I laughed at that, suddenly feeling awkward with his hand on my shoulder and looked down at my feet. I had a strange desire to kiss him, but reminded myself that he was a widower. I looked down at my feet, swallowing the lump in my throat. He seemed to remember the pain of losing his wife so strongly; I wasn't sure how to compete with that.

"Hey," he said softly, trying to get me to look at him.

I did, trying to muster a smile. It felt sad on my cheeks.

"It's going to be okay." He pulled me in for a hug, and I leaned my head on his shoulder, wrapping my arms around his waist. It was nice to be held, and I took a deep breath, enjoying the leathery scent of his clothes.

Eventually I pulled away, feeling awkward. I wanted more from him, but how was I supposed to tell him that? I'd never really been in a relationship, I didn't know how to approach them. I'd been on dates, but none of them had been important enough to take time away from my research. I just hadn't cared. Now that I was starting to, I didn't know what to do with myself.

I cleared my throat, trying to shake those thoughts from my head, and looked at Chester. "Okay, I'm ready. How do I get to the Beyond?"

Chester nodded and turned away from me, settling onto the floor and gesturing for me to sit across from him. I did, careful not to let our knees touch. He started to explain how to make a key to open the gates. It was hard to concentrate, but I thought of Jana sitting next to me in her prison, and it was easier. I still had to save her.

"Remember when I told you my cairn allows magic to become physical?" he asked, reaching up to touch the stone.

"Yes. It's how you make your sword," I replied.

"Good. It's also how we make keys. Each gate has a specific key. Your cairn will know how to make the key, but you must remember what it looks like or your cairn can't make it real."

"My cairn is a she," I said when she made a huffing noise at Chester calling her an "it."

He looked at me, his eyebrows lowered. He shrugged, and reached behind him to a folder full of papers. He pulled out six sheets, each with a detailed drawing of a key.

"These two," he said dropping a couple pieces of paper to the side, "we won't worry about yet. Those are the gates between reality and the spirit world, and since you're going to confront him here, you don't need them."

There was no key to my reality, and I was only mildly disappointed to have that confirmed again. Three gates between the spirit world and home, but I would only ever be able to get halfway.

Chester held out a drawing of a white key with jagged teeth that reminded me of a lion's mouth.

"This is the first one you need to memorize. You must hold an image of it in your mind while you use the magic of your cairn to create a physical copy," he explained.

"How come we don't just get keys?" I asked, wondering why it had to be so difficult.

"Do you want just anyone to be able to travel between realities?" he replied, raising an eyebrow.

I shook my head quickly, turning the drawing in my hand and trying to memorize the pattern of teeth.

I got it, my cairn whispered, supplying an image of a three-dimensional key in my head.

Really? I asked, surprised. If I turned the page over I wouldn't be able to remember how many teeth there were.

Yes, she snapped, sounding irritated.

"My cairn says she remembers," I said, feeling awkward.

Chester nodded, his brow furrowed, reminding me, once again, how strange my relationship with my cairn was. He didn't question me and held out his hand. In his palm there was a green, glowing key made of Chester's magic that matched the picture perfectly.

"You can pick it up to look," he said, reaching forward so I could take it.

The key was warm and smooth under my fingers. It wasn't very big, just the size of my palm.

"I've never held someone else's magic before," I said, holding the key up to my eyes.

"You held my soul, so this shouldn't be too weird for you." He chuckled, his eyes glinting. That made me blush, and I smiled despite myself.

"How do I make my own?" I asked, trying to stay focused.

"Magic is always physical. You pick up items and

make physical changes to the world," he explained, sounding like a teacher. "The difference between this type of energy and the kind you're used to is that now you're actually creating something out of your energy, something that could survive without you around."

I nodded, adjusting my legs underneath me and leaning forward.

"The cairns make it possible to shift magic from energy into a physical object. All you have to do is keep a picture in your mind and push the cairn's magic toward that image. If it helps, you can make a ritual or spell, but I've always just used visualization. You must remember to absorb the energy back, otherwise you run the risk of someone else getting a hold of your key."

I nodded, seeing the wisdom in that.

I can do it! My cairn said, sounding so smug I had to roll my eyes at her. She didn't like that, supplying me with an image of her sticking her tongue out.

"My cairn says she can make it." I handed back his key, and started gathering energy from the opal stone. My cairn was bubbling with excitement, eager to show me what she could do.

She supplied the image and I focused on it, pulling the power from the ring and focusing it in my right palm. I imaged the weight of the key in my hand and the smooth feeling of the bone. With an audible pop, the key pressed against my skin and I closed my fingers around it.

Chester held out his own key, and together we looked for any differences.

"That was impressive," he said, turning over my replica and studying the teeth. "It took me three weeks to make a toothpick."

I smiled at the praise. My cairn was practically

purring.

"Now make sure you can absorb the energy back. Just close your fist around it and think of it sinking back into your magic."

I did as he instructed. At first, all I managed was to dig the key into my skin and pinch myself. I shook the pain away and took a deep breath, finding my calm center. I treated the key like a power source, just like my sapphire or the cairn, and siphoned the magic out. The key crumpled in my palm, disappearing as though it had never been.

"Very good," Chester said, and then moved on to the next key.

We practiced for a couple hours, rotating through the keys. Once I was able to create all of them, Chester started testing my memory by matching each key to its respective gate. The exercise was mentally exhausting and I hadn't even tried to open a door yet.

"Opening the gates is the easy part," he assured me when I asked about it. "Once you remember the key, all you have to do is think of a door with a keyhole."

I thought about it for a moment, then asked, "What if we opened the seventh gate from this reality?" It would be easier if there was a way to skip the gates in between.

"The amount of energy required to open four gates at once would cripple your magic. You'd probably lose the soul that you're guiding, maybe even yourself," Chester explained. "Each gate requires energy to maintain while you walk through, and trying to hold even two open at once would be catastrophic."

I nodded, but I still wanted to try.

Maybe not yet, my cairn said, her voice concerned. *Let's wait until we have more practice before trying advanced techniques.*

I smiled at her words, agreeing with her assessment.

"Okay, let's try the first gate. Bring Jana with you. We can go to the Beyond now," Chester said, standing up and holding out a hand to help me.

"What? Now?" I asked, scrambling to my feet without his help before bending down to scoop up Jana's vial.

"Who knows what Drekvic is out there doing," Chester replied, shrugging his shoulders. "The faster we manage this, the faster we can stop whatever he's planning."

My heart was pounding in my head, making it difficult to think. I swallowed the lump in my throat and took a deep breath.

"Okay, I'm ready."

I thought of the teeth-like key again and was just about to push it into existence when there was a knock on the door. Concentration broken, my cairn's magic sparked angrily and stung my fingers. I quickly pushed it back into the ring to keep it from causing more trouble. I rubbed my hand while my cairn apologized.

Chester walked to the door, looking through the peephole before sighing heavily. He opened the door and Rakshina walked in without invitation.

Her long legs crossed the room in two quick strides. She stopped next to me and smiled. After holding her soul, I couldn't help but smile back. Chester, of course, was not amused.

"What are you doing here?" he growled.

"I came to make sure you didn't need any help. I've recovered from my earlier shock and find that I am unable to sit still," she replied, putting an arm around my shoulders and leaning to look in my face.

"You want me to help, right, Ellie?"

I laughed as Chester shut the door, walking back to us with heavy steps.

"She can already make all the keys. We're taking her sister to the Beyond now," Chester explained.

"Lovely. I will not interrupt." She mimed zipping her lips, and I had to purse my lips together to keep from giggling. Chester looked murderous, but turned back to me and told me to continue.

The first key came easily, and as Chester had promised, conjuring the door was simple. It amused me that I imagined the thick green door of home, and was comforted to see it again--at least I was until I opened it.

I staggered as the energy required to tear open a rift in the fabric of reality hit me. My cairn quickly sent me a rush of power, bolstering my resources. Chester didn't let me hesitate, grabbing my arm and pulling me through the door. Rakshina followed and shut it behind us.

The crippling drain of energy subsided, and I took a moment to catch my breath before looking around. I could still see Chester's living room, but it was in gray-scale. The edges blurred and hurt my eyes if I tried to focus on them. It was also completely silent; my breath was deafening.

Chester's golden aura was a bright beacon in the dim light. It was a stark contrast to Rakshina's soul, a black hole in the muted world. If I didn't trust her, it would have terrified me.

"Don't linger," Chester said, his voice sounding oddly muffled. "Keep moving forward. Open the next gate."

I nodded. The fifth gate was a four-sided key made of metal. It seemed harder to bring it to life in this reality, as though there was something in this dead space that opposed creation. By the time I was able to force it into my hand, sweat was beading on my forehead and I felt like I had just run a mile.

I was afraid to open the door again, but at Rakshina's urging, I conjured up the image of my front door and opened it again.

My knees buckled as the rift sucked power from me, and I only just staggered through it. Chester and Rakshina followed, both looking unconcerned and calm.

We repeated the process for the sixth gate, and by that time, I was completely spent. This area was plagued by a cold wind and completely devoid of any recognizable shapes. Chester's living room was gone, and the Beyond, even though it was only behind one more gate, was invisible to us.

Rakshina looked unimpressed by my sweaty face and heavy breathing. Once through the sixth gate, I had collapsed in an ungainly heap on the marble-like ground, trying to catch my breath. Even my cairn was quiet, trying not to show how exhausted she was.

"There's only one more, Ellie," Chester said, kneeling down next to me. "You can do it."

"No," I panted, "I can't." My limbs felt heavy and my brain sluggish. I couldn't even remember what the key looked like, much less figure out how to drag myself through the door.

"If we aren't here to help you, you're going to have to do this with a struggling siekewa by yourself," Rakshina said, her voice loud to be heard over the wind that bit our faces.

"This is only the first time she's tried," Chester admonished, giving Rakshina a dark look.

"I made it through my first time," she snarled back.

"You'd been traversing the realities for a hundred years before you were a collector! You can't expect her to do the same."

I wanted them to stop arguing, but I was too tired to care. I just wanted one of them to open a gate and get us out of the wind.

"She just needs the right motivation. If saving her precious little sister is not enough, we have to think of something else."

I didn't like the sound of that, and I reached for my shoulder bag that held the vial of Jana's soul. Chester didn't like it either, and he stood up with his hands on his hips, facing Rakshina like an angry tiger.

"We will just try again. Stop being so pushy."

A devilish grin spread across Rakshina's face as an idea came to her. My eyes widened and I tried to struggle to my feet, worried about what she would do. She reached out and tapped Chester's forehead before he could react, like a snake striking at an enemy.

A spell burst from her fingers, and Chester's knees buckled. I lunged, trying to catch him. My arms felt like lead, and the best I could do was to keep his head from hitting the ground.

"Get him to the Beyond or he's dead," Rakshina said, and with a snap of her fingers, she vanished, leaving me alone in the swirling wind.

Dread made it difficult to breathe. I had trusted her and she had left me here in this in-between place that Chester had warned me was dangerous. It was easy to lose yourself here, and the power of the spaces could easily drain your magic until you had no chance to get home.

"Shit," I hissed, panic settling in. My cairn wasn't doing much better, running through all the keys, wanting me to try all of them.

"I don't know if I have enough energy to make one, much less all of them. Stop freaking out," I snapped, trying to get under Chester so I could figure out the best way to drag him.

My cairn fell silent, letting me think. I could feel her, hovering like a concerned mother. My hands were trembling, but I blocked out the screaming wind and the exhaustion telling me to lie down and rest. I pretended I was in Chester's living room, and he was showing me the pictures again, one key for each gate.

I went through them, one by one, until I got to the dark violet skeleton key that didn't match the doors I'd used already. My cairn jumped with glee, ready to try.

The key was easy enough to manifest, but I was afraid of the final door. I didn't know how long I could keep it open. I imagined the door and inserted the key, hesitating only a moment before opening it.

I fell to my knees. It felt like claws were digging into my flesh, tearing me apart and asking for more. I was crying with the pain, but I grabbed Chester's arm and struggled to my feet. They slid on the smooth floor as I started dragging him along.

Rakshina jumped through my open door and put an arm around my waist. She grabbed Chester's other arm, and supporting both of us, she pulled us through to the Beyond.

I looked at her when we were through, swaying lightly on my feet with tears streaming down my face. I wanted to hit her, but she just smiled at me.

"You did it, Ellie, all by yourself," she said like a proud parent.

My knees felt like noodles and I slumped to the ground, the world going black. I felt the moment Rakshina slammed the door shut, but I was too far gone to care.

CHAPTER FIFTEEN

I took a deep breath, enjoying the taste of the summer air in my lungs. The pollen would have made me sneeze back home, but in the Beyond, allergies didn't seem to exist. A breeze ruffled my hair and cooled the skin on the back of my neck. It was time to stop procrastinating. I had work to do.

Rakshina told me that if I couldn't calm Jana within five minutes, Hope would kick her out of the Beyond, and she would be lost as a ghost. It made an already difficult task even more terrifying, and I was exhausted from the trip.

I had been using more magic in the last few days than I had in the past year. As a teacher and a researcher, most of my magic was used for academic study and demonstrations. The spell might be powerful, but it wasn't something I did often. Since becoming Fate's replacement, I was practicing constantly with major magic, but if I didn't do this now, I might not get another chance.

Chester had gone for a walk and would return soon. He'd be surprised if he came back and found me still sitting here, not having completed my mission. My legs felt like lead as I pulled myself to my feet. It was going to happen. Now.

Strengthening my resolve, I set Jana's vial in the middle of the gazebo. The Beyond would provide whatever I wanted, similar to Chester's dresser, so I requested a piece of white chalk, holding my hand out and watching it fall into my fingers from thin air. Relaxing my clenched jaw, I knelt down next to Jana's vial and started to draw. As I drew the spiral, I allowed my magic to flow into the chalk, turning it a gentle sapphire. I continued walking and drawing until I hit the edge of the gazebo. I stretched my back as I stood, looking at the faintly glowing lines.

I crossed back to Jana, careful not to step on any of the lines. I kept my breathing even as I picked up her soul. The magic would be working with my breath, so it was important to breath mindfully. The steadier I was, the more powerful the magic would be.

I stepped on the first loop of the spiral and felt my breath hitch. There was a fierce tugging on my soul trying to pull me into the bottle with Jana. My cairn's power flowed around me, cutting me off from the tug. I forced my breath out of my lungs, and then back in, steady as my heartbeat.

I started walking the spiral, each step careful and exact. I kept pouring my magic into the chalk until the light turned the gazebo blue. I wanted Jana to become aware surrounded by my power. Hopefully, it would be familiar enough to stop her from struggling against it.

Each step was difficult. I could feel my own magic wanting to pull away from me as I walked. I had always known that spirals were powerful tools, but I had never tried to channel one this big. My only contact with them had been to pull out viruses when I was sick, and those only used a small fraction of power. I'd never walked one before and certainly never one in such a magical place.

One deep breath in, one long exhale out.

I was close to the edge when I felt something heavy drop onto my chest, squeezing my lungs so violently I couldn't breath. My magic hiccuped and sputtered and my cairn flared to life, screaming her battle cry.

It was the weight of Drekvic's power, the stopper that kept Jana in the vial. I had known it was coming, so I let loose my reserves, flooding my body until I felt like I was on fire. My skin was glowing and my hair was floating straight up in the air, charged with static. I took another step and a gasping sob of air.

With each step the weight on my chest got heavier, trying to choke off my breath completely. I kept demanding more power from myself, pouring out all I had just to keep walking. I was gasping, my heart was beating erratically, but I had to finish.

My foot finally touched the last point of the spiral, and Drekvic's magic shattered. The vial in my hand did as well, cutting my palms. I collapsed to my knees, unable to stand any longer.

My cairn threw out her power, encasing us in a large silver bubble as Jana's soul exploded from her confinement, violent and angry. She hit the edge of the bubble and I felt the impact vibrate through my bones. She jumped off, coming back toward me. I could feel her spirit, confused and hurt, surrounding me and trying to break into my mind. She had been trapped and used without remorse, and she wanted to fight back.

"Jana! Stop!" I cried, my tears sounding loud in my voice. I pushed my magic to fill the bubble created by the cairn. I put all the love and hope I could into it, wanting Jana to know that I loved her and would do anything for her. I had to calm her or Hope would send her away. I refused to let that happen.

Sister? I heard her ask in a wavering voice.

"I'm here," I replied, gasping a little. Relief threatened to overwhelm me, but I forced myself to stand and look at Jana's wisp of a soul in front of me.

It slowly took my sister's heartbreakingly familiar shape. Her blue eyes were full of tears and fear made her beautiful features ugly. She looked so small.

"I'm so sorry," she whispered, falling to her knees and sobbing.

I knelt in front of her and pulled her to me, hugging her as fiercely as I could without hurting her. I stroked her pillowy hair and kissed the top of her head, tasting the salt of my own dried tears.

"Oh, sweetie," I whispered, rocking her back and forth. "I was so worried about you. It's okay now."

"I shouldn't have done it, Ellie. I shouldn't have trusted the siekewa," she sobbed, hiccups interrupting her words. "He said it wasn't important, but it is! The cairn is a soul. I almost gave him a soul!" She held onto me as though I were the only real thing in her world. In a way, I was.

"It's okay. You're safe now. You're in a safe place."

Her words sunk into me and I felt sick. Jana had stopped it, but I hadn't. I had given Drekvic the soul he wanted. What did that make me?

"Where are we?" Jana asked after several long moments. She pulled away from me and looked around the gazebo.

I wondered how she saw it, if she could see the magic pulsating in the air or feel the souls in the distance enjoying the sun. I wondered if she felt at peace.

"The Beyond," I replied.

"I'm dead," she said, looking like she might burst into tears again.

I nodded, quietly.

She couldn't look at me as she pushed her hair behind an ear and stood up. She turned away, clasping her hands together in front of her. I stood as well, letting my own hands fall to my side even though I wanted to touch her again.

"That's probably for the best," she said finally, turning to look at me with watery eyes. "How's Mom?"

I winced. "Probably not good. I… had to leave her to save you. If I can go back, I will, but I don't know how."

"You have to try," Jana insisted, grabbing my shoulders and shaking me. "You have to—how did you get me away from him?" She let go of me, her eyes going so wide I could see the whites around her irises.

"I had to make a deal with him," I said, wincing at the words.

"What did you promise him?" She grabbed me again, her fingers digging into my upper arms.

"I gave him a cairn," I replied, looking at her chin to avoid her gaze.

She let go of me as though it burned. Her jaw clenched, and she raised her fists as if ready to fight me.

"How could you do that, Ellie?" she shouted. "Don't you know what they are?"

My chest began to boil. My skin felt hot and my vision blurred. My fingers cramped and trembled.

"You!" I hissed, my anger leaking into my words.

"I did it to save you!"

"You put my life above countless other souls that are going to be *destroyed* because of him!"

I met her eyes, unrepentant.

"And I would do it all again, Jana! You're my little sister. I'd chose you every time."

I stalked away to the other side of the now blackened spiral, empty of magic and will. My hands were stinging and I realized I still had shards in them. I swore and started pulling them out, the sound of their wet clicking on the floor as I dropped them seeming louder than it really was.

"I'd do it again and again," I snarled, irritated that she was judging me. She still hadn't said anything, so I kept going. "I'm going to fix it. I'm going to stop him, but—I had to free you first. If something happened to me, I didn't want you to be stuck in that vial."

I jerked my cardigan off, ripping it to bandages to wrap my hands. They stung fiercely, but I relished the pain, letting it fuel my outrage.

I knew what I had done was wrong. Jana was only one life, and even knowing what the cairn could do, I gave it to Drekvic to save her. I tried not to think about how that decision made me a murderer.

Jana's arms wrapped around me as she came to rest her head against my back. I felt her sigh as she relaxed into me. I used to hug her like that when she was upset about a boy.

"I know you will," she said softly. "You're good at that. I'm sorry, Ellie. I messed up. I never should have made that deal with him in the first place. I just—I wanted to be good enough to be your little sister."

"You're an idiot," I said, smiling with my voice. "You're the best little sister in the world." I turned around and put my arms around her shoulders. She rested her head on my chest and sighed again.

"Thank you for saving me."

"You're welcome," I replied, stroking her hair and closing my eyes. Hugging her again, comforting each other, it brought me back home, to a simpler time, when I didn't have to worry about anything so terrifyingly important.

Chester cleared his throat quietly, but it pulled me instantly back to reality. Jana was safe in the Beyond. Drekvic couldn't reach her here, and that was all I had ever really wanted. I had other things I needed to do now. There was a price for Jana's safety, and that meant I had to leave her, probably for good.

She turned to look at our intruder, taking in his black leather and intense expression as he studied her in turn. I knew he was looking for signs that we were related. Jana's sun-kissed skin and blonde curls were a far cry from my pale skin and dark auburn hair. She was strong, with defined muscles from years of running and swimming. Our faces were similar, with the same rounded shape and small noses, although our eyes were different colors. I wondered if Chester would even notice the few similarities.

"It's a pleasure to finally meet you, Jana," he said, giving her a gentlemanly bow. He stayed standing just outside the gazebo on the steps. "My name is Chester. I've been helping your sister."

"You're a collector." Jana moved in front of me, her shoulders tensing. "Ellie has to go back home to our mom. You can't have her soul yet."

Chester met my eyes and raised an eyebrow.

I put a reassuring hand on my sister's shoulder and walked around her, wanting to be between them.

"Fate assigned him to help me after I stupidly went

to the spirit world before I was dead," I explained to her. "He saved my life when I first arrived, and he's been helping me ever since."

I was glad my cairn was a ring instead of a necklace like everyone else's. I didn't think Jana would be able to stomach it if she realized what I had become. She would know I'd never be able to join her here in the Beyond, and I wasn't sure how she would react to that.

"So he's your friend?" she asked, wrinkling her nose at the thought.

"Yes, he is," I replied, nodding.

She crossed her arms and I could see her shoulders relax, if only slightly.

"If you've been helping my sister, I guess I won't hurt you."

"I appreciate that," Chester said, giving her a winning smile. Well, it was meant to be winning. Jana had other ideas.

I almost laughed, remembering how sour Chester was when he first met me. He had been so annoyed and frustrated at the fact that I was alive, furious with Fate for having misled him.

"Ellie, I got a message from one of the other collectors. There's going to be an emergency meeting. We have to go," Chester said to me.

I turned to Jana, feeling sadness well up inside me. I didn't want to leave my little sister. I wanted to stay with her and talk, connect like we used to. I had to move forward, and knowing Jana was safe where Drekvic couldn't touch her was comforting. Even so, I didn't think I would ever really be ready to let my sister go.

I rushed forward and hugged her. She returned the gesture, her arms almost too tight.

"I'll miss you," I whispered, unable to help myself.

"Don't come back until it's your time," she hissed back at me. "I love you, Ellie. I know you can fix things."

"I love you too, Jana. I promise I'll make everything right again." I didn't promise I would be back; she'd be able to hear the lie in my voice.

She nodded and I pulled away from her. I took one long, last look at her angelic face, memorizing it. I would do everything in my power to follow her wishes. I would try to return to our mother, but I would look at the cost now. I put millions of souls at risk for Jana. I couldn't do that twice.

I kissed Jana's forehead and turned away.

Chester put an arm around me and took us back through the gates to the spirit world. I didn't look back.

CHAPTER SIXTEEN

The cairn hall was packed, and benches were pulled from all sides, full of collectors. I felt immediately like I couldn't breathe, the anxiety in my chest pulling tight. I was worried that I was going to be the cause of this gathering, but it wasn't something I could run away from. Chester pulled me to the side and we managed to find a space where we could both sit.

The room was loud and full of energy, most people seeming to not know what was going on. I overheard two collectors behind us talking about the rise in humans falling into comas and their souls disappearing. I worried if Drekvic had already figured out how to use his cairn to take souls. He hadn't had a teacher, but if he'd been able to take Hope's magic and splinter realities, it was a safe bet that he was smart enough to figure out the cairn on his own.

Thomas dropped down beside me, too close for comfort. I almost flinched into Chester on my other side, and then tried to sit up straighter, adjusting myself and hoping no one noticed.

"Still shining so brightly in our spirit world," he said to me, smiling.

I managed a faint smile back, and thankfully that was all that was required, because there was a soft gong that echoed through the room, drawing all of our attention toward the center. I turned away from him, trying to hide the cairn on my hand without being obvious about it. I turned her gently so the stone rested against my palm.

Hey, she hissed at me, sounding offended.

I don't want to have to explain that I've taken Fate's place. What if they recognize you? I asked, and then sent an image of angry and scared collectors. I heard her sigh, and then settle into the back of my mind. She wanted to listen, but I had muffled her ear piece. I would just have to deal with the slight intrusion. I almost nodded consent, but stopped myself before Chester or Thomas asked what I was doing.

The collector who rang the gong was one of the elders I had seen at the festival. He looked young to me, with bright green eyes and brown hair, but his seniority was without question as the room fell silent. He seemed to be the unofficial leader. He stood with his hands on his hips and his feet slightly spread. It was an aggressive stance that demanded loyalty and trust. I would have to ask Chester what his name was; I was sure I'd have to speak with him soon.

"The siekewa, Drekvic, has a cairn and is using it to steal souls from humans and other creatures before their time," he said, his voice carrying through the room. I was sure he was using magic, because with so many bodies in the way, words wouldn't be able to echo and carry as they did otherwise.

Whispers broke out with his statement, and Chester reached over to take my hand in a comforting gesture. I squeezed his fingers, appreciating it.

"Two of our collectors, Rose and Marshal, have disappeared this week. I have been unable to trace them using their cairns, so they can't be in the spirit world or the Beyond. I believe the siekewa must have taken their souls and cairns for his own use."

I noticed Rakshina leaning on the wall near the front of the room with easy access to the door if she needed to leave. She touched the cairn around her neck and closed her eyes. She looked upset, and I noticed other collectors glancing at her, hostility in their gaze.

"The only question at this time is whether or not we can stop the siekewa and save those souls, or if we will only become victims ourselves."

"We can't just sit and do nothing!" a female collector in the front called out, fire in the way she sat forward in her seat.

"But if he catches our souls, how will we guide others?" another asked.

The woman started arguing, but I tuned her out. The last thing I wanted was to stand up in front of all these seasoned collectors and tell them about my plan to stop Drekvic, but I needed their help. Someone would need to take the souls from me once I stripped them from the siekewa. I knew I couldn't hold all of them at once, especially because they'd be fragile from misuse. They would be upset, and the thought of letting even one of them fall through the cracks was too much.

Gathering my bravery, I stood up. I saw Chester shake his head, unwilling to let go of my hand. I turned to him when he wouldn't let me go forward.

"I need help," I whispered. "I don't want anyone else getting hurt because of me."

He looked worried, but nodded and let me go. I

knew he was right behind me when I walked to the edge of the building and walked forward. He waited by the wall instead of coming to the center with me, but I stopped before entering the elder collector's space. The room had gone eerily silent when I approached the center.

"You don't need to concern yourself with collector matters, child," the elder said, looking at me kindly.

"Yes, I do," I replied, holding out my palm so he could see the cairn there.

The elder flinched back, looking horrified. "Fate! This is why I couldn't find her? What have you done?" he asked, angrily.

"She gave me her ring and left," I replied. I didn't care if anyone else heard me, only the collector in front of me was important at the moment. "She wanted to be with Hope, and she thought I would be a suitable replacement.

He studied me, his green eyes unsure and the youthful line of his mouth hard and straight. Finally, he nodded, and stepped aside, letting me walk to the center of the room.

I took a deep breath and turned to face the collectors. Some eyes held hostility, while others looked confused. They didn't understand why I was in front of them, and I had to put my hands on my hips to keep myself from fidgeting.

Being a teacher, I was used to lecturing and speaking in front of crowds, but I was always safe in the knowledge that I had the most authority in the room. I was the new Fate, but I didn't have their loyalty. That was something I had to earn on my own. I turned to look at Rakshina, grateful for the calm in her gaze. I turned around again to find Chester smiling encouragement. Despite all the other collectors around me, I had two that I could trust who trusted me in return.

Friends, Ellie. Those two are your friends, I heard Jana whisper in my ear. It wasn't really her, but something that she would say to me when we were younger. I was comforted by the memory.

"I gave the siekewa his stone," I said, using magic to carry my words across the room. I didn't put much power into it, not wanting to force conversations to stop.

I felt them take a breath of outrage, but I plowed on, knowing that if I stopped I would drown in the chaos.

"I gave him the stone to save my sister's soul, not knowing what he'd do with it. When I went to Fate for help, she gave me the power to stop him. I've been practicing with Rakshina and Chester, and I can do it, but I can't do it alone. I need your help. All of you."

"Why should we trust you?" It was the same woman that had told the elder they couldn't sit by and do nothing. I could see her eyes now, alive with a righteous fire. She believed the collectors were powerful and could protect the souls on their own. They were *her* charges and she, understandably, didn't like me.

"You don't have to trust me," I replied, standing up straight and imagining I was talking to a rowdy classroom instead of immortal souls. "You just have to have faith. Fate believed I could do this. She believed in me so much that she left to be with her lover in the Beyond. If you go after Drekvic on your own, or even with the other collectors, you *will* fail. He'll just steal your souls and take your cairns."

"Child," the elder said, stepping forward to command my attention. "He will just do the same to you , and your cairn is more powerful than ours. It would be even more dangerous in his hands."

"When I made the deal with him to save my sister's soul, he made me a promise. He can't steal my soul unless I willingly give it to him or his powers will be stripped. Those are the laws he made to govern his siekewas, and so he must abide by them as well."

There was silence while the collectors thought about it. I knew I had to win their help here, or I'd have to do it on my own. If this didn't work, I'd be at square one again, with no idea how to fix the mess I'd made. Rakshina looked like she wanted to say something, but she held her tongue. If the first one to speak for me was a siekewa herself, no one would listen.

Thomas stood up, a look of determination on his face. I was afraid of what he would say, and wondered if he would speak for me or against me.

"I will follow our new Fate," he said, tipping his head to acknowledge me.

The silence stretched on after his words, as collectors turned to their neighbors, questions in their gaze. The elder put his hand on my shoulder, and when I looked at him, he nodded.

"As will I," he said, not projecting his voice, but the gesture was clear for all to see. It was a domino effect from there, and soon all the collectors were standing up around me, talking amongst each other about the upcoming trials. I was tense, and I didn't like being called the new Fate, but I needed their help, so I wasn't going to disregard their words. Being Fate meant I'd have to lead them, at least until she returned. Chester moved to stand by my side and smiled at me.

"The new Fate, huh?" he asked.

"I'd rather not," I replied.

"You'll do fine. Were you ever properly introduced to Samuel?" Chester gestured to the other collector still standing with me, contemplating the group around us. He looked up at his name, and gave me a tight smile.

"I'm Ellie," I told him, holding out my hand. I knew his opinion was important, and I was grateful that he'd spoken up for my plan.

"Yes, Fate told me," he said, shaking my hand. "You really think you know what you are doing?"

"I'd like to think so," I replied, nodding. "I've been practicing with Chester and Rakshina."

"Rakshina is a good collector, despite her dubious origins," Samuel said, looking over to where she had been standing. She had left the hall, uncomfortable with the press of people around her. "She showed you how to take a siekewa's soul?"

"I can do it, but I have to take his power source first. All those souls will need to be brought to the Beyond, or put back in their bodies if taken recently. I won't be able to do that, steal his cairn's soul, and take his to the Beyond. It's too much for one person."

Samuel looked aghast at the mention of the cairn, so I nodded confirmation.

"It's the only way to stop him. If the cairn wants to return to its the stone, I'll put it back, otherwise I will take the cairn to the Beyond as well. I just have to take one step at a time."

"He's moving quickly. He needs to be stopped before he gluttons himself on the world. The panic in your reality is already rising," Samuel said, still clearly uncomfortable that I could steal a cairn's power.

"Then let's get going."

CHAPTER SEVENTEEN

Drekvic was moving through Asia. Its dense population helped him steal the most souls while traveling the shortest distance. Chester explained that they were able to track Drekvic's movements because all collectors could sense souls. If I kept practicing, I would be able to sense when souls were dying as well, and I would be drawn to those I was meant to collect. As Drekvic's victims fell, their collectors were dragged to that place by the absence of their chosen souls. Drekvic may as well have been firing flares into the sky.

I didn't want the collectors, especially not Chester, getting too close. The last thing I wanted was for him to be hurt—or worse. He had already done so much for me, and despite my best efforts, I cared about him a lot.

The plan was for Chester to drop me off somewhere in the spirit world, and I would call Drekvic to me there. I still had his name, so I could request his presence. It was his decision whether or not to come, but I knew he would. He had claimed to want me for his lover. He would come when I called him.

The area that Chester had chosen was perfect. It was an open field with tall grass and a blackened spiral at its center. The spiral sat on a rough, flat rock sturdy enough to stand on. The field was isolated enough, but the collectors could still reach me when the time came.

My palms were sweating as I surveyed the field and the residual magic left in the rock. I had to succeed or all those souls would be lost. If Drekvic wanted access to the Beyond, it would be on *my* terms. He had to know that his family was safe, but I had to keep everyone else safe, too.

I noticed Chester standing in my peripheral vision. He walked over and stood next to me, looking out over the waving grass.

"You're going to be okay, Ellie," he said, brushing his fingers against mine. "The rest of us will be just out of his sensing range, but I won't let him hurt you. I promise."

"I'm not worried about the help," I replied, trying to give him a smile. It was flat and insincere on my cheeks. "I'm afraid that I'll fail and all those people will be lost because of me."

"You can do it," he replied, taking my hand in his and squeezing lightly. His touch surprised me, and I stamped down the emotion rising in my throat. He had loved someone else a long time ago, someone he had left and lost. I wouldn't share my feelings. "You're going to be okay."

The new smile I gave him was genuine despite my heart fluttering in my chest. His firm palm against mine made me feel light-headed. I pulled away reluctantly before I did something stupid, turning away to look across the field towards the trees where the collectors would be hiding.

"I will call him soon. Is everyone ready?" Chester pulled a small shell from his jacket and held it up to his ear, listening.

My heart was so full watching him. I knew that he'd do anything to keep me safe, to keep his promise. I was glad that Chester was on my side, even if only because of Fate's orders.

"They're waiting on Rakshina to get into place," he said, interrupting my thoughts.

"I wanted to say something to Ellie first," she said, her voice coming from right behind me. I jumped and whirled around to face her.

She looked stylish and somber in a dark gray, knee-length dress, bright against the pitch black of her tights and leather ankle boots. Her pale blue eyes were full of an emotion that I couldn't quite name, framing the visible lines of worry between her eyebrows.

"Ellie," Rakshina started, biting her lip and looking down at her feet. "I know you want the collectors to take the souls where they belong, and I want to help, but I think I'm better equipped to help you with the siekewa instead. Chester has a better touch with distressed souls than I do and I can open the gates just as easily as him. I think I can help hold the siekewa's soul while we drag it through."

"Why didn't you mention this earlier?" Chester asked, annoyed.

"I don't like to talk when there are many collectors about. They look down on me despite the last two-hundred years proving myself!" she snapped, her eyes flashing with anger.

"I don't want to leave Ellie with you. You could strand her in the gates."

"And she could have let me go to become a ghost," Rakshina snarled, stepping closer to Chester. "I am tired of being doubted and treated like a leper. I am a collector, just the same as you, and Ellie is my friend, just as she is yours. You have nothing to base your doubt on aside from what I *was*."

Chester looked frustrated, but remained still. He didn't want to listen, but Rakshina made sense. If she was guiding me, she'd be able to help hold Drekvic's soul.

"It's going to be dangerous, Rakshina," I said, stepping forward to get between them. "If I can't control him, he could steal your soul."

"Chester's would be more easily stolen than mine," she replied.

That settled it for me. I hadn't liked the thought of risking Chester's soul, but if he was off collecting souls, I could concentrate properly on Drekvic. Besides, if Rakshina was right, Drekvic would have a hard time with her soul.

"Chester," I said, turning back to him. He looked angry, but waited for me to finish. "Rakshina has a point. If she can help me with Drekvic's soul and will be safer doing it, then I think it's best for her to stay with me."

He sighed and ran a hand through his hair. "Rakshina is right in that I have my prejudices, but even so, I won't leave you unprotected. Fate told me to keep you safe. I have to stay by your side."

So he was only protecting me because of Fate's orders; my chest felt like I'd been crushed. I had hoped he cared for me as well, but all of his kindness was on Fate's behalf. It didn't make any difference, I still wouldn't be able to concentrate if he were hurt.

"Then both of you can stay, but you have to stay back." I put my hands on his chest and gave him a slight push. "If something was to happen to you..." I shrugged, unable to finish the sentence. I didn't want to reveal how much I felt for him.

"I'll be fine," he replied. "I am not defenseless."

"I know."

"We should take our places," Rakshina interrupted, stepping towards the edge of the rock and looking back at Chester. "We will join Ellie here once she has taken the souls from the siekewa, and we will stay as the other collectors take them from her. Chester will open the gates to the Beyond. I will assist Ellie with holding that bastard."

With that, she jumped lightly off the rock, vanishing before she hit the ground.

Chester turned towards me and gave me a tight hug.

"Stay safe until then," he whispered. I nodded against his chest, suddenly too nervous to speak.

He kissed the top of my head and stepped away, vanishing the same way Rakshina did. I paused, wondering why he had kissed my hair. Surely that wasn't obligation, was it? I shook the thoughts away. There was no time for sentiment.

I had to summon Drekvic.

I opened up my magic, pouring it into my voice as I whispered his name, knowing without a doubt that he would come.

"Drekvic, we need to speak," I whispered, feeling the magic tear the words away from my lips and throw them into the world, racing to find him.

CHAPTER EIGHTEEN

The air suddenly became cold. I shivered, glad that I wore my gray sweater and jeans. I stood up straight, willing myself to stay strong. The sky became dark with clouds, that seemed to appear out of nowhere, bending and stretching into dark, angry beings. The wind lifted the hair off the back of my neck, and I turned around slowly to make sure that Drekvic hadn't appeared behind me. That was when I saw the first snowflakes drift toward the ground.

The rock underfoot somehow repelled the snow as it fell, forming a perfect circle around me. I took a step toward the edge, wondering what was happening. If Drekvic was strong enough to control the weather, did that mean I was, too? Could I change the world around me as easily as he did? It made me wonder, but I'd have time to find out. At least, I hoped I would.

"Ellie," Drekvic whispered, and I whirled around to find him standing on the opposite side of the stone wearing his usual black clothes. His blue eyes reflected the sky and seeing him, I realized how insane my plan was. Drekvic was stronger than anything I could hope to be, and I was planning on taking his soul?

My mouth went dry and I wanted to run, but I couldn't. I'd made a promise to stop him, and I had told Jana I would succeed. I couldn't give up, no matter how badly I wanted to flee.

"Drekvic," I replied, taking a step forward. I wanted to be in charge of this conversation. "You can make it snow, huh?" I mentally kicked myself. He would never believe I called him just to chat about the weather.

"Yes, ever since you gave me that lovely stone, I have been able to control many things," he replied, smiling. "Besides, the water in the air will dampen sound, and keep all your lovely collectors on the outskirts in the dark about our conversation."

I tried not to let his words register on my face. I had wondered if he'd be able to sense them and anticipate the trap. I'd just have to improvise.

"You came anyway," I said, taking another step closer. I was standing in the middle of the stone, and he was on the opposite side. I'd gone halfway. For this to work, I needed him to trust me. I needed him to come to me.

"I told you how I feel about you, Ellie. I will come whenever you call me, nefarious plotting aside." He took his first step, starting to close the gap between us.

"You're the nefarious plotter here, Drekvic."

"But you plotted to save your sister's soul. You snuck into the heart of the collectors' territory and took a stone for me. And now, I suspect, you are trying to stop me from taking more souls."

"Yes, I am," I said, proud that my voice didn't waver. "It's not just to save the souls though. I want to save *you*."

He scoffed at that, crossing his arms defensively. "I don't need saving."

I broke my own rules and stepped closer to him, taking a step sideways so I could start to walk around him. I kept my head up, careful to keep him in my line of vision, without openly staring.

"I know you're trying to save your family. You created the realities, and now you're trying to reunite your parents so they can be together again."

He laughed, turning to face me like I wanted him to. I stopped on the rock's outer edge with an eyebrow raised and my hand on my hips, trying not to look petulant as he lingered toward the center.

"The elder has been telling his stories again?" Drekvic asked. "He always wanted to make me seem better than I am. Maybe that was the way it started, my sweet girl, but now that I have this power, I can do *anything*. Once I have enough power, I can tear down the barriers between the realities. Don't you want to go home to your mother? I could make that happen for you."

"Why do you want to tear down the gates?" I asked, suddenly wary. He was offering me something I wanted, trying to manipulate me into doing something. I remembered our first deal and wondered if I could use it to my advantage. If I made a deal, he would be forced to get close to me, and I could take his power. I didn't see the cairn, but his ruby ring held a sinister glow.

He combined the power sources, my cairn whispered to me. *His cairn's soul is in there. He put it in a spiral.* She sounded scared, but determined. I mentally nodded, letting her know I understood without alerting Drekvic.

It was hard to look at him with my cairn's fear rolling around me, but I made myself do it. Drekvic needed to let his guard down before I could stop him. I took a slight step forward, noticing Drekvic draw back. He didn't want me to get to close to him. That was interesting—was Drekvic afraid of me?

"If there's only one reality, then there's no need for collectors. I'll be able to access all the souls in the Beyond as well, and with the power of three cairns..." he let his voice trail off and then shrugged. "I'd be stronger than my father."

"And that's what you want? Why?"

"I have my reasons. Why would I tell you?"

"Because you want something from me," I said, moving forward again. I moved enough that he would have to actively take a step back to distance himself, and he wouldn't do that. He wanted to be in control of this meeting, so he wouldn't retreat. "You knew this was a trap," I continued, "and yet you came. You want something from me." We were only a few feet away from each other now. If I moved fast he'd be within my reach.

"I want you to ditch the good girl attitude and join me. Our powers together would be unstoppable." He came to me, closing the distance between us and entering my personal space. He put an arm around my waist, pulling me closer to him. "I want you to be mine," he whispered, his voice low and rough.

His touch sent ribbons of power through me, but I refused to let it overwhelm me. I held onto them, savoring their strength and taking them as my own.

He was so close that I could feel his breath on my nose and smell the deep ash scent that clung to him. I wanted him to think he had me. I relaxed into him, pressing myself against his chest and wrapping my arms around his neck.

His magic leaked into me, and I held it, allowing it to burn my skin and create rivers of fire up and down my spine.

"Have you changed your mind?" he asked, his voice suddenly rough. Hope and hesitation lit up his pale eyes, and I almost felt guilty for deceiving him. He was tired of being alone. I was going to save him from himself.

"I'm going to help you," I replied, leaning forward and brushing my nose against his.

At the same time, I reached out with all my magic and asked his captured souls to come to me.

No amount of practice could have prepared me for the chaos of emotion his prisoners brought with them. My cairn flared to life, trying to protect me from their anger. I doubled over, fighting to stay in control.

Drekvic shoved me away, trying to break the flow of souls, but it was too late. Thousands of them swirled around me, my cairn creating a calm pocket of energy in the hurricane of their rage.

I straightened myself, turning to face Drekvic with my hands balled into fists. His eyes were wide and his teeth bared, looking nothing like himself.

"You're making a mistake," he threatened.

With so much power at my disposal, I doubted it.

"You can fight or let me help you. Either way, I'm going to win," I said, feeling the presence of the other collectors as they started swooping in to take the souls.

I let them, focusing all my attention on Drekvic. Someone as old as the world itself didn't need souls to have more magic than I did.

"Oh, Ellie," he said, his voice thick with emotion. "We could have been so good together."

He threw his hand out as if to catch something and I was thrown forward as he tried to pull on my soul. Our contract kept him from succeeding, but the familiar magic made his souls scream. The sound startled my cairn into dropping the bubble around me, allowing Drekvic's magic to wrap around my waist and lift me up.

His pale eyes were cold as he pulled me toward him. I didn't look away as I prepared a strike of my own. There was no way I was strong enough to best Drekvic, but as my practice with Chester had shown me, my magical touch hurt—a lot.

Using my cairn's power along with my sapphire, I reached out to brush his soul. He hissed in pain and dropped me. I managed to land on my feet, already moving forward to rush him before he could recover.

I tackled him, grabbing his wrists and rolling onto the stone. Sharp rock dug into my knees as I pinned him on the ground. Still pushing against his soul, I jerked the ruby ring off his hand, feeling sick as it caught on his nail and tore it.

I started building the bubble around us, preparing to pull his soul from his body as he frantically tried to shield himself from my power.

Something slammed into my shoulder, sending me flying across the stone. My arm burned as bits of dirt and rock found their way through my sweater and scraped against my skin.

I scrambled to my hands and knees, finding the ruby ring where I had dropped it and snatching it up. I staggered to my feet and turned back toward Drekvic.

"Rakshina!" I shouted, starting to rush forward across the stone.

She had shoved me away and was struggling with Drekvic, a silver knife in her grip. I recognized its dark aura from her house. She was trying to kill him, cursing wildly. Tears were streaming down her face as she stabbed down blindly. He managed to evade and wiggle away at the last moment, but she finally got into his guard, leaving a bloody gash along his cheek.

He snarled at her and started gathering a blast of power. She wasn't even trying to protect herself, so intent on stabbing him that she was blind to all else.

I lunged at her, rolling her away and throwing up a bubble around us just as Drekvic's magic released. The force of his spell buckled my shield and I frantically pushed more energy into it, trying to make it hold.

"I'll kill him," Rakshina hissed, anger rolling from her body.

"Help me!" I shouted, kicking her in the shin as she struggled to sit up.

She grunted and glared at me. Her eyes blinked rapidly, as though she was coming back to herself. She noticed my crumbling bubble, the only reason we weren't dead, and put a hand on my outstretched wrist.

Her magic flooded into me and followed the path of my own spell. Our shield exploded outward, pushing aside Drekvic's magic and scattering his remaining souls. I prayed that the collectors would be able to gather them all in time, but I didn't have a moment to worry about them as the recoil of the explosion pushed me back into the rock.

I heard the sickening thump as Drekvic landed in the tall grass.

Chester appeared almost on top of me, his feet on either side of me as I looked up at him form my back. He shoved Rakshina aside with his foot, making her moan in pain as she rolled over onto her stomach.

He reached down and took my wrists, easily pulling me to my feet. Once I was standing, he touched my face his hands snarling in the loose hair around my ear. His relief that I wasn't injured was apparent in the way that he brushed the dirt off my shoulders.

"Fate help us, Ellie. Are you hurt?" he asked, even though he could clearly see that I was more or less uninjured.

"I'm fine," I insisted, trying to pull away to make sure Drekvic was down. Rakshina certainly was, crying like a madwoman and cursing Drekvic's soul in multiple languages. I'd feel sorry for her later. She had compromised everything.

He still has a cairn! My stone screamed into our connection, her panic as evident as the swirling white magic gathering behind Chester's back.

Get it away from him! I hissed back at her, struggling to jerk Chester behind me. He didn't understand and moved too slowly. I threw out my hand, allowing my cairn's power to rush forward and find Drekvic's stone. She stopped suddenly, her power burning my fingers as it ricocheted back into me.

Chester grunted, his knees buckling as he fell. I caught him while I watched in horror as his golden aura leeched from him, flying toward Drekvic's open palm. I used my magic to lower Chester gently to the rock, stepping between his body and the siekewa.

Drekvic dropped Chester's soul neatly into a vial and stoppered it, holding it up with a grin on his face.

"I warned you not to fall in love," he said, his voice sounding almost like his old self. The blood dripping down his face and the wild disarray of his hair belied his confident tone.

"Let him go." I enunciated each word like a snarl as I stalked forward.

"Why should I?" he demanded, throwing the vial up in the air and catching it again. The edge of my vision blurred as my fury rose to the surface. If he hurt Chester with his carelessness I would kill him and scatter his soul into the in-between.

"Give me my ring and I'll let him free." Drekvic shook the vial by the stem, the contents flaring with golden light.

We have to get Chester's soul back to him before his body dies, my cairn hissed, her worry flooding me with urgency.

If I gave him the ring he'd have enough magic to disappear. I couldn't let him get away with a ring and another cairn.

I can't find it, my stone wailed, sensing my question before I asked it. *He's hiding it from me. It's weak because he's been draining it to fight you. It makes it harder to see.*

A small sob escaped my lips before I could stop it, my heart breaking. If I couldn't get Drekvic's cairn by stealing it, I would have to barter for it. Drekvic had two things that I wanted.

"Give me Chester's soul and the cairn, and you can have your ring back," I said, taking another step forward and flashing the ruby at him.

He laughed maniacally and I fell still, the sound raising goosebumps on my arms.

"I'm not stupid, Ellie," he snapped. "You can only have one or the other."

I'd promised myself I wouldn't make impulsive decisions anymore. I had to weigh the consequences of my actions, and Chester's soul wasn't worth the power of a cairn, even a weakened one. Tears stung my eyes and I swallowed the lump in my throat.

"He's trying to turn you." I jumped as Rakshina's raspy voice spoke in my ear.

"What?" I asked, glancing at her briefly before turning back to Drekvic. I didn't want to turn away from him.

"If you choose the cairn, your guilt and hatred of yourself for letting Chester die will change you into one of us, fueled by all the stray magic in the air here," she explained, her voice low so Drekvic couldn't hear.

"I'm waiting!" he shouted, his voice cracking. He had climbed back up onto the stone and was tossing Chester's soul into the air again.

Found it! My cairn screamed at the same moment Rakshina exploded beside me, her magic lashing out like a whip and shattering the glass prison. Drekvic cried out in surprise and covered his face, protecting his eyes from flying glass. With hundreds of years of practice, Rakshina plucked Chester's soul out of the air before Drekvic could react. She pulled it to her and disappeared from my side, rushing back to Chester's still form.

I didn't let Drekvic recover, throwing my hand forward again and letting my cairn's power loose as she rushed to Drekvic's cairn. He had it reset in an ear piercing, wearing it backwards to hide behind the fold of his ear and the messy halo of his dark hair. My cairn pulled the soul free from the stone, cradling it in her grasp and bringing it to me.

Without anything I wanted from him, Drekvic turned and ran, jumping off the stone and limping through the grass toward the trees. I didn't immediately follow him, turning back to Chester and kneeling down, to place the cairn's soul gently into Rakshina's hands.

"I've got Chester. Go after him!" Rakshina shouted, angry at my hesitation as she juggled both souls. Chester was propped up in her lap as she struggled to calm his panicking soul enough to get it back into his body before he died.

I touched Chester's face briefly, not liking how

cold his skin was. I leaned forward and kissed his cheek.

"Don't you dare die on me," I whispered in his ear, my voice stronger than I felt.

I stood up, meeting Rakshina's pale gaze. "If you let anything happen to him..." I said, letting my words trail off with the implied threat.

"Get the hell out of here!" she snarled, angry that I was breaking her concentration.

I nodded, and even though my heart was breaking, I jumped off the rock into the snow-kissed grass.

CHAPTER NINETEEN

It was cold and wet, soaking my jeans in moments. It was still snowing, and if I hadn't been running as fast as I could after Drekvic, I'd be concerned about the weather. As it was, it took all my willpower not to turn around and make sure Rakshina was taking care of Chester. She seemed like she knew what she was doing, but after her stunt with Drekvic, I wasn't one-hundred percent sure I could trust her.

The path was easy to see. Drekvic was running ahead of me and crushing a trail in the long grass. I could just make out the back of his coat in the gloom as he reached the edge of the field and entered the trees. I pushed myself harder, feeling my legs burn in a familiar way. I could almost picture Jana running just ahead of me, telling me to keep up and push myself or all those cookies I ate would find a home on my thighs.

The memory gave me strength, and I pushed forward. Drekvic was weakened now, but he wasn't an idiot. He still had his own power, and anyone that could hold a portion of Hope's strength without buckling under the weight had to be packing a hefty arsenal of magic. I reached the edge of the grass, stumbling into the darkness of the trees.

Drop! My cairn shouted at me, and I listened, lunging toward the ground. I saw the branch whistle over my head. Drekvic had been waiting for me, hidden in the darkness. I rolled away from his feet and jumped back up, ready to face him for round two.

I had no martial arts training, and if he was planning on fighting me with punches and kicks, I was probably going to lose. He swung the branch at me again and I backpedaled, falling on my butt. He was furious, and it was the first time I had seen him lose his composure. He wasn't handling his loss of power very well.

I made a face as he took another swing at me— Drekvic may have lost his power source, but I still had mine, and I was going to use it. I raised my hands and pulled energy from my sapphire, pushing Drekvic away with a wall of air and magic. The invisible assault caught him off guard, and he stumbled back.

I scrambled to my feet, gathering more magic into my eyes so I would be able to see if he tried anything. My attack had pushed him to the ground, and as the air dissipated, he looked up at me from his kneeling position with pure hatred in his eyes.

"You have no idea what you've done," he hissed, his voice trembling with rage. "They were almost free!"

"You don't need to save them!" I shouted back at him. His hands were starting to fade in a black cloud of magic, so I told my cairn to be ready with a shield. She confirmed, and I felt her gathering her own power inside of me. "Fate's in the Beyond right now, waiting for you."

"Liar!" He threw his magic at me. It slid across the shield my cairn created, trying to snake around it to reach me.

My first instinct was to make a bubble, but if I was fighting off his magic in a bubble, Drekvic could just run away. I didn't want to have to chase him again. I wanted to end this struggle now. Taking a deep breath, I took a chance and pulled down the shield. I opened myself up and when Drekvic's magic hit me, I tried to take it as my own.

It felt like eating dirt, but I held onto it as it tried to incapacitate me. It was nice of him not to launch a killing blow.

You're mine now, I growled to the power, forcing it to curl into a ball in my palm. I looked up at Drekvic, feeling my hair start to float.

He was staring at me with his jaw agape. It would have been amusing, except for the utter fear in his eyes.

"What did you do to my mother?" he whispered, his voice full of pain and loss.

I didn't deign to answer. Fate had done this to me.

I sent my cairn's power out to trap his soul in a large bubble around us. Her magic was glowing a fierce white, and it lit up the dark forest like a beacon. Drekvic cringed, looking away from the glow. I used that opportunity to reach out and speak to Drekvic's soul.

It recoiled, just like Rakshina's had, but there was something different in it. Drekvic's soul was broken, and the jagged edges stung.

Please, let me take you home, I whispered to him, and his soul uncurled, trying to resist my call. It was sullen and unhappy as it left his body. He slumped to the ground as I cupped his soul in my hands, asking my cairn to help keep him contained. She closed a bubble around Drekvic's soul, buffering me against him.

Drekvic's soul was twisted. The edges were jagged and folded in on themselves. The core was still intact, and it throbbed with one purpose. All the blackened pieces, Drekvic's willingness to tear down anything that stood in his way, were a result of that purpose. I thought of my burning need to save Jana and wondered if my soul would have eventually looked like his.

I couldn't afford to be blind to the consequences of my actions anymore. I wouldn't let Drekvic do it anymore, either. I stood up, cradling his soul against my stomach. All I had to do now was get to the Beyond on my own. This was going to be fun.

Drekvic's soul was already pushing against the sides of my cairn's bubble. He couldn't resist my request, but he wasn't going to make it easy on me. I took a deep breath and started creating the first key.

I set the tooth-like key into my mind and used my cairn's magic to make it solid. I could feel her stress. She was struggling to hold Drekvic while making the keys. My own magic couldn't take physical form, but maybe I could help her hold Drekvic.

I wrapped my magic around her and started weaving it into her bubble. I made sure to match the textures to keep the bubble strong, tightening each thread and clipping away any weak points. With that done, I turned back to the key in my hand. My cairn sent me a tendril of gratitude for the support.

We imagined the door, the familiar frame appearing in front of us. I unlocked it, pulling it open. I didn't give myself the luxury of crying, even though the energy required to open the gate bit into me like a wild animal. I stepped through and closed the door as quickly as possible.

I imagined us climbing steps to get closer to the lights in the sky. I couldn't see them because of Drekvic's storm, but I knew they were there, and I had to keep reaching for them. With each step, we got closer and closer, and with each gate the spirit world faded.

Drekvic fought me. He hadn't fulfilled his purpose and he refused to give up. He slammed his magic against our bubble, digging the edges of his soul into us. It hurt. I had to stop twice to repair the damage, giving more and more power to my cairn until I felt thin and weak.

We were at the last gate when he managed to punch a hole in the shield. His soul started to claw its way out, and my cairn's magic, exhausted, vanished. Without her magic filling in the weaves, our prison was broken. Drekvic was loose, and his soul was gathering, ready to attack.

If we were lost here in the windy in-between, there wouldn't be any moving forward. He couldn't get out without a cairn, and mine was so tired it was hard to say whether or not I could get out either. I drained my sapphire, pulling all my power into me.

My hair stood on end, flowing in the currents of magic and my skin glowed a brilliant blue. Even my cairn had turned blue from the magic in the air. I reached out and snatched Drekvic's soul in my hand, crushing him into submission. I knew he was probably screaming in agony, but I was done. He was causing so much pain for no reason. Enough was enough.

I demanded the final key from my cairn. I knew she had nothing left, but I had thought that about myself only a moment ago. We were almost done, and I wouldn't let her quit on me. She dropped it into my hand. It was a dark violet key, vibrating with my magic. I didn't have time to conjure the door from my mind. Instead, I shoved the key into the fabric of the Beyond, seeing the shadow-shapes ahead of us. The door appeared without any effort. I shoved it open and threw Drekvic through, sliding in behind him before slamming it shut.

My magic leaked out of me all at once, and I collapsed on the cool, manicured grass. This was it. We'd finally made it to the Beyond.

CHAPTER TWENTY

I awoke to the sound of happy crying and the sweet smell of dirt and grass. I blinked, trying to make sense of my splitting headache and the deep ache in my arms and legs. I could barely make out the shapes around me and I didn't know why I was on the ground to begin with.

"Ellie," a familiar female voice whispered. Hands pushed me onto my back. I winced in pain, trying to focus on the pale figure above me.

"Chester?" No, it was Rakshina. She was supposed to be with Chester, it was important. Why was I suddenly afraid?

"He's fine," she said, brushing my hair out of my face. "You really messed yourself up, didn't you?"

"Did I make it?" I asked, remembering I had shoved Drekvic through the gate. I had followed and collapsed on the grass. Before that... there was the wild chase, and then before that... Chester was dying.

I sat upright, instantly regretting the decision. My vision tilted and spun, and my stomach cramped. I felt sick, but I had to know. He had to be alright.

"Where is he?" I asked, painfully forcing myself to my feet.

Rakshina reached out to steady me, gesturing to Drekvic's prone form several feet from me. Fate was leaning over him, her hands glowing. The crying had stopped.

"No," I said through clenched teeth. I was *not* about to be sick. "Where is Chester?"

"He's resting. He shouldn't travel until his soul recovers. Here." She placed her hand on mine and shoved some of her power into me. Immediately, the headache started to subside and the world stopped spinning.

That's right, I thought, remembering parts of my fight with Drekvic. He had left me magically dry, making me weak. I was still sore, but I had faith that those aches would fade eventually. I gave Rakshina a small smile. She rolled her eyes, and then gestured with her chin. I looked over to see Fate walking towards us.

I tried to not lean so heavily on Rakshina, but then I saw my cairn. I cried in dismay at the beautiful stone, cracked into two pieces. I desperately looked for her soul, but the energy Rakshina had been able to spare was barely enough to reach her. I could feel her fear, holding onto her existence by a thread.

I wanted to cry. I had no magic left to help. My headache was already returning as Rakshina's borrowed energy began to fade. I looked up, panicked as I cradled the broken stone in my hand.

"It's okay," Fate said, surprising me. I had forgotten she was there. She reached out and cradled my hands in hers, flooding me with power. "Help her."

I nodded, using Fate's borrowed power to delicately lift my cairn's soul as she whimpered, small and frail. I wanted to pull her out of the broken cairn, but her ties to it were too tight. I slowly started cutting them away, each slice bringing her closer to reality and farther away from the stone. Some pieces were tangled in the shards of the cairn, so I mended that too, wishing it was easier. By the time I held her trembling soul in my hand, the cairn was whole again, but empty.

Holding her, I realized that I could fulfill my promise and release her to the Beyond. Fate was still supplying me with magic, so I used her power to soothe my cairn. When she was calm, I tried to release her. She would take her original form instead of being the powerhouse inside the cairn.

No! She cried, trying to stop me. Hearing her voice again was a relief, even if her words didn't make sense. *We are a team now. I don't want to stay here.*

I made you a promise, I told her, not understanding her resistance. She wanted freedom, didn't she?

I want to stay with you. Put me back.

I looked at Fate, unsure. She seemed to understand, because she pulled my cairn's soul to her and, with a surge of magic, dropped her into the empty stone. It flared to life and I was taken back to that in between place to strike a new deal.

My cairn threw herself at me in a fierce hug.

You stupid girl, she cried, holding me tightly. *I was so worried about you.*

It goes both ways, I replied, hugging her back. *I can't believe you want to stay here.*

I want to stay with you. You are my friend, and I haven't had one of those in a very long time. I will stay with you as long as I am wanted. You will never require a new cairn.

I pulled away and smiled at her. *And if you ever want to rest, you better tell me. Are you sure you don't want to stay in the Beyond? You'd be happy here, and I did promise that you could stay.*

I will be just as happy to stay with you. She
seemed to think for a moment. *Ellie, can I ask a
favor? I never had a mother to name me, so I've
chosen one for myself, Can you call me Joy?*

I smiled again, unable to help myself. As the in-
between space began to disappear, I felt Joy's
presence comfort me; it was nice to not feel alone in
all of this. I looked up at Rakshina and Fate, making
sure my cairn's ring was securely on my finger.

Fate released my hand. She had given me enough
energy to keep myself stable. Her smile was angelic as
she put her hands behind her back.

"You saved him. For that, I cannot thank you
enough," she said.

Rakshina grunted, turning away.

"I'm going to check on Chester," she said,
disappearing with a soft pop of displaced air.

"She hates him, doesn't she?" I asked, feeling my
relief slowly start to disappear.

"He took Rakshina from her family and raised her
as a monster. Her life goal has been to destroy him.
My son has only made enemies," Fate said, sighing.

"Is he okay? I'm afraid I wasn't as gentle as I
could have been. I got... annoyed."

"He is sleeping now. He will wake up when his
psyche has healed. You did well."

"Good. I need to sleep," I said, feeling exhausted
all over again. I had done the impossible, and all I
wanted to do was curl up and go to bed.

Suddenly remembering, I pulled out the ruby ring
from my pocket and shoved it toward Fate, glad to get
rid of it. Fate took it and nodded.

"I have one more thing to tell you," she said,
giving me a mischievous grin.

I didn't want any more surprises, especially from

Fate. She must have noticed the irritation on my face, because she laughed.

"You are strong enough to open the first gates and return to your own reality."

I took the small object she held out for me, a regular house key. A key that changed everything. I could finally go back home. I held up the key, my fingers trembling. Joy studied it as well, assuring me that she had already memorized its shape and size. She gave me the magic to create a duplicate, and soon I was holding a glowing white key next to the mundane silver one. I didn't know what to say.

"Those who fight for me are always rewarded. Thousands of souls are free because of you, including someone I love very much."

"Thank you," I whispered, excitement bubbling over the exhaustion.

Fate waved her hand to open a portal in front of us and I could see the spirit world beyond. She had opened four gates at once without even blinking. Through the portal, I could see the flower garden in front of the lake where I had first appeared. I could go home from there.

I hesitated. "I haven't said goodbye."

"Chester will find you. Don't worry," she said, raising an eyebrow.

I flushed, embarrassed that she had known exactly who I was talking about. If he could find me, I could go home and still see him again.

Grinning, I jumped through the gates.

CHAPTER TWENTY-ONE

Three Weeks Later…

Otherworldly crying had drawn me to a lonely stretch of dirt road. It was old and neglected, with huge potholes that were too much for my little electric car. I parked off the main highway and spent at least twenty minutes walking down the road. Chester could have teleported me from the spirit world, but it would have left me too tired. Going back and forth between realities was still exhausting, and it would be awhile before I felt comfortable using that much power.

The area on either side of the road was overgrown farmland, damp with the recent rain. It was gloomy, with gnarled branches and weeds trying to eat the road. The crying child wasn't much farther; I could hear him louder now from around the next bend. I side-stepped a large hole and saw the little boy just beyond.

Sandy blonde hair stuck out form under his black riding cap. His light gray pants were dusty from a fall, and his leather boots were scuffed. His round face was bright red from crying, and I couldn't tell the color of his scrunched up eyes. He was small and abandoned, and my heart instantly broke for him. His words were hard to understand between his cries, but he was calling for his father.

Chester was waiting for me. His eyes were locked on the little boy. He didn't notice my arrival, his jaw set and his eyes brimming with emotion. I wondered how many times he had come to this spot, trying to make his son see him. The thought hurt, and I wanted to go over and comfort him. I decided to start what I'd arrived to do without disturbing him.

I wanted to ask for his permission before approaching his son, but I would have to open up the lowest gate in order to speak with him, and it was too much of an effort. We had talked about this several times, and I already knew it was okay to at least try. I was confident I could wake ghosts up enough to collect them, but I hadn't yet tried with any this old. Fate claimed that the farther they were from their time of death, the harder it would be to wake them up to their own reality.

I knelt down in front of the child, blocking out my surroundings to focus entirely on him. He sang with such pain and fear that I could taste it in the air. It was the reason these fields had been abandoned. They couldn't thrive under so much emotional stress.

I pulled magic from my sapphire and blew it toward the child. I curled it around his eyes, trying to penetrate into his thoughts. *See me,* I commanded, giving the magic a small push.

Sniffling, he blinked and looked up, squinting as though he'd never noticed the world around him. He'd been lost in his own misery for so long that he'd forgotten a life outside of it. Even so, I had wanted him to see me, and that's what he saw first, his father's eyes staring back at me in confusion.

"Hello, Michael," I said, smiling at him.

"Who are you?" he demanded, his voice hoarse from years of wailing.

"Your father asked me to find you."

"You know my father? Where is he?" His little face scrunched up again, tears flowing all over again.

I brushed his damp cheek, pouring more magic into him, hoping I had not wasted too much time trying to make contact. *See him,* I said, pointing at Chester.

"He's right there, Michael. He's been looking for you." The boy's eyes widened as he screamed in relief, running as fast as he could to Chester's open arms.

Chester scooped the boy up, holding him tightly. He was crying as he kissed his son's hair. They were talking to each other, but I couldn't hear a word. Once a soul accepted its death and awoke to its reality, it passed through the first gate. I couldn't interact with them now unless I followed. Chester looked up to meet my eyes. I couldn't hear him, but I could read his lips.

"Thank you."

I stood up, smiling. They were fading as Chester took his son to the Beyond. I dusted the dirt off my pants and began the twenty-minute walk back to my car.

It had been three weeks since I returned to my reality. I had dropped into Melo's back room, where she told me I'd been gone for seven days. My mother had been furious, but I told her I'd just needed time alone. I apologized and slept at her house for a few days to keep her calm. Work had just assumed I needed more time to process Jana's death and didn't mind my absence.

My own house felt empty, even with Joy to keep me company. I was always alone, unless I was with my students or talking to Chester.

Chester, I thought his name, feeling my chest tighten. I accepted how I felt about him, but I wasn't willing to take the next step. Chester was finally able to take his son to the Beyond. Perhaps he would remember his wife, and want to keep her memory sacred. There was no way I could tell him how I felt now.

I was done making impulsive decisions. My actions had consequences that I couldn't ignore. The entire ordeal was exhausting, but at least it had taught me to consider what might happen in the future instead of just solving the most immediate problem.

I had only been walking for ten minutes when I realized the birds had stopped singing. I slowed, looking around at the overgrown fields trying to find what had silenced them.

I stopped, turning to look down the road. The way was clear, if a bit ominous from the low-hanging clouds. I hoped it wouldn't rain. I turned back, wanting to get to my car before it started, but I was drawn to a halt at what suddenly stood between me and the distant highway.

Fate was smiling and waving, and next to her was Drekvic. I wanted to turn and run. Nothing Fate brought to my life was for the best, but curiosity got the best of me. Drekvic looked like a completely different person. His signature black clothes were replaced by dark blue jeans and a green t-shirt. His hair was messy around his familiar face. There was something off about him, though, and I realized his pale eyes were no longer blue, but a golden brown surrounding a thin ring of green. He looked annoyed and suspicious. As he should be, with Fate around.

"Hi, Ellie!" she called, waving at me again.

I crossed my arms and waited. I still had millions of ghosts to collect. I definitely didn't have time for whatever she wanted me to do now.

She grinned and gestured to Drekvic, barely able to contain her excitement. "Well, tell her!" she cried, actually clapping.

He rolled his eyes and looked at me. I felt a shiver run down my spine, and I just knew I wouldn't like whatever came next.

"I'm your new roommate," he mumbled.

Nope, I didn't like the sound of that at all.

Acknowledgments

This book and this story has been apart of me for almost four years now. I've shared it once before, but it wasn't quite complete. I hadn't put all the pieces together yet, so I took it down and I'm starting again, and I have so many people in my life that made this possible.

This trilogy is dedicated to my mother. I told her I was never having children, so the only grandchild she will get named after her will be a character in a book. Thankfully, she thinks that is just as cool.

I'm also grateful to my editor, Andrew, and the other member of our writing trio, Kasey. I never knew that playing a video game would introduce me to so many great writers and wonderful people. Andrew has taken this story above and beyond what I could make it by myself, and for that, I'm eternally grateful. Kasey told me, up front, that one of my ideas was a train wreck waiting to happen. Thank all the heavens that I listened.

I'd also like to bow down to my best friend and beta reader, Leslie. I always hold her opinions in high regard when it comes to telling me whether or not a story is worth reading. Like always, her insight has made this book better, and that's good for all of us.

Warren Designs created this amazing cover, and I cried when I first saw it, literally.

And finally, thank you to my wonderful partner, Phil. There were so many times in this journey that I had to put off things while I finished working, and many hours spent apart because I needed the space to be productive. But he stuck with me, and his love and support and random acts of kindness are the reason I'm still here.

Hey, Thanks!

Thank you for reading the first book in my trilogy! You would be my hero if you could review this book on Amazon or Goodreads! The importance of reviews for independent authors cannot be overstated, as it allows us to get exposure and make a living doing what we love. It takes only a couple minutes, and it makes a HUGE difference.

Wayward Hope, the second book in the *Wayward Gods Trilogy* is coming out in May of 2019. If you want to get early chapter previews, sign up for my mailing list at http://ldgreenwood.com. You'll get emails from me twice a month with sneak peeks, book reviews, and, of course, more information on releases. It's a lot of fun and I love it when my readers interact with me.

Thank you for all your support, and I hope you're looking forward to hearing more from Ellie, Chester, and Drekvic in May 2019!

Love,
L.D.

Made in the USA
Lexington, KY
31 July 2019